THE
GARRISON

K. Sean HARRIS

THE GARRISON

All Book Fetish titles are available at special quantity discounts for bulk purchases for sales promotion, premiums, fund-raising, educational or institutional use.

Cover concept by: K. Sean Harris

Cover Design by: Sanya Dockery

Book Design, Layout & Typesetting by: Sanya Dockery

Published by: Book Fetish
www.bookfetishjamaica.com
info@bookfetishjamaica.com

Printed in the U.S.A.   ISBN: 978-976-610-839-7

For they eat the bread of wickedness, and drink the wine of violence.
PROVERBS 4:17

Again, they are minished and brought low through oppression, affliction, and sorrow.
PSALMS 107: 39

Prologue

"**G**o suck yuh madda!" the youth growled menacingly, pulling a 357 magnum from his skinny waist. The object of his wrath, a taxi driver old enough to be the young man's grandfather, saw his life flash before his eyes. And for what? For having the audacity to demand payment for taking the youth and his friend from Cross Roads to the outskirts of the notorious community innocuously known as Rosewater Meadows. Only taxi drivers that lived in the community dared to venture there after dark. It had a very violent reputation.

"Alright, alright," the taxi man said, trying to placate the irate youth. No sense in dying for a hundred and fifty dollars. "Everyt'ing criss."

The fourteen year old youth, known as Bambino to everyone in his community, smirked at the taxi driver. He relished the fear he saw in the man's eyes. He felt powerful. At that moment he was God. It was his decision whether the man lived or died.

"Today ah yuh lucky day old boy," he told the man, as he chuckled and placed the gun back into his waist. Still chuckling, he and his companion walked nonchalantly across the street.

The taxi man watched them as he tremblingly lit a cigarette, inhaling deeply. He just couldn't believe how violent the youths of today's Jamaica were. All they cared about were guns, clothes and women. Hell some of them didn't even care about women. The gun and the power it wielded seemed to be the ultimate orgasmic experience. When his heartbeat returned to normal, he turned the car around and headed back to Cross Roads. He would pick up any passengers that were going in his direction but that would be it for the night. He was going home to his common-law-wife and their three kids.

And thank God for sparing his life to see another day.

Chapter 1

The community of Rosewater Meadows hadn't always been a fecund whore that bred criminals and cold-blooded killers who contributed significantly to the country's spiraling murder rate.

As recently as fifteen years ago, it had been a poor but proud, God-fearing community. The pastor of the lively and influential Tabernacle Baptist Church was the acknowledged community leader and moral voice of the community. In those days, only one murder had taken place in the community, and that had been a crime of passion.

Benjy, a street vendor who earned a meager living selling cigarettes, box juices and dry fare such as bun and cheese, animal crackers and sandwich biscuits, had heard rumours that Nose, so named because of his unusually large nose and who was said to also have another unusually large body part, was having sex with Marjorie, his common-law-wife of eight years, while he was away.

Benjy had dismissed the rumours initially. Not his Marjorie. She was a very devoted Christian woman. Never missed church on Sundays, unless she was ill. Cooked, cleaned and took care of him and rarely complained about anything.

She was a good mother too, their five year old son Alton, was always clean and wasn't as rude as most of the children his age in the community. So he had not paid any mind to the dreadful, malicious rumours. People were just jealous of his happy home, he had surmised.

But the rumours persisted like an annoying mosquito that always came back no matter how you tried to swat it away. Tie that in with the fact that Marjorie had been feeling a bit loose lately when they made love, Benjy became a troubled man. One Friday morning, he decided he would prove to himself that the rumours were not true, and that the supposed 'looseness' of Marjorie's vagina lately, was due to his mind being influenced by what people were saying.

On that fateful Friday morning, he left their small, two room board house at his usual time but instead of heading to East Queen's Street where his stall was located, he went over by the old railway station about a mile from his home, and enjoyed a spliff while sitting in the shade of a Julie mango tree a few meters away from the abandoned station. An hour later, he got up and made his way back home.

Miss Lucy, a fifty-eight year old woman who spent most of her days at the neighbourhood grocery shop gossiping with Yvonne, the owner, was sweeping outside her gate when Benjy walked by, heading towards his home. He told her a pleasant good morning and continued on his way, humming an oldies hit by John Holt.

Miss Lucy, having seen Nose pass by a mere fifteen minutes ago, dropped her broom and ran as fast as her stumpy, arthritic riddled legs could take her down to Yvonne's shop. This was too exciting to keep to herself.

Benjy arrived at his home, located in a yard that consisted of three houses. The only difference between the houses was the colours. Benjy's was painted in blue while the one directly beside it was white and the other had no paint. One of his neighbours, Marie, was by the side of her house, washing as usual. She had six kids, none older than eleven, and seemed to spend most of her time doing laundry. She looked at him with her eyes wide. She nodded back a hello, seemingly unable to speak.

Benjy heard the sounds as he climbed up the steps. His bed was squeaking the same way it squeaked late at night when he had sex with Marjorie after Alton, his son, had gone to bed. The other sound was not so familiar. Marjorie, *his* devoted Marjorie, was uttering words and making sounds that he had never heard in the eight years he had been with her.

Bloodclaat Nose! Yuh nah go lef' some fi mi man? Eeh? Pussyclaat! Yuh ah fuck it like ah fi yuh pussy! Ahhh! Ahhhh! Mi pussy deh pon fyah!

Time stood still for Benjy. An observer would have thought that he was a mannequin. He had even stopped breathing. His brain struggled to process what he was hearing.

Ugh!Ugh! Bumboclaat! Lawd Nose yuh big wood ah go kill mi! Oh God! It hat but it sweet nuh rass! Fuck mi Nose! Yuh nuh si how it wet? Fuck mi kill mi Nose!

Benjy's emotions ran the gamut from shock to disappointment to blind rage.

They shifted with the ferocity of a race car driver neck and neck with a rival on the home stretch of a championship race. He retraced his steps, eyes riveted on the door, as though he could see everything that was happening inside. He stumbled down the steps and retrieved his machete that was leaned up against the wooden wall just underneath the bedroom window. The squeaking had gotten louder, like the bed was under even more duress. Her screams had gotten louder too. More intense. Nose was really fucking her into tomorrow. *His* woman. His *devoted, Christian* woman.

Woi! Mi ah dead! It ah go come through mi throat! Nose! Nose! Jesus God Almighty!

Benjy couldn't take it anymore. He moved quickly now, adrenaline pumping so hard he could barely breathe. His chest felt tight. His legs felt light, like he was floating on air. He opened the door.

They had been so caught up in their passionate love-making that neither of them saw him at first. Marjorie was perched on the edge of the bed, facedown on her knees with her thick legs spread wide. Nose was behind her sweating profusely as he gave her all he had, which was a lot, and as hard as he could, which was pretty hard. The sight of Marjorie taking such a hard pounding from such a mammoth dick and *loving* it; froze him for a few seconds.

Nose saw him first.

"Bumboclaat!" he shouted in fright as Benjy, with tears in his eyes and murder in his heart, attacked him with the machete. The first chop separated Nose's left wrist from

4

the rest of his hand as he raised it in desperation to ward off the chop.

He screamed in agony as blood gushed from the open wound like a scene from a horror flick.

Marjorie's screams were deafening as the blood from Nose's hand sprayed her like a fire-hose. She scampered out of the house naked, bloody and screaming, as Benjy mercilessly continued to hack Nose's body to pieces.

Marjorie bolted through the large crowd that had gathered in the yard and ran down the street, too terrified and traumatized to be concerned about her nakedness. When the police came, Benjy was still chopping. The scene was so unbelievably barbaric and grotesque that one of the four cops who had arrived on the scene, a grizzly thirteen year veteran of the force that had seen a lot in his time, fainted upon entering the room.

Benjy was given life in prison, and died two years into his sentence. Many said it was from a broken heart. Marjorie had left the community the following day. She went back to her family home in Bethel Town, a rural district in Westmoreland.

The community had spoken of nothing but the tragic incident, which had also dominated the news nationally for a few days, for a very long time. They had never experienced anything like that before. The community had been shaken to the core.

If they had been told that one day, in the next fifteen years, their beloved community would become one of Kingston's most notorious garrisons; and atrocious acts would occur on a regular basis that would make Nose's murder pale in comparison, they would have laughed in disbelief.

But those days have indeed come.

Chapter 2

Barack Obama had just created history by stoutly defeating John McCain in the United States presidential elections to become the first African-American president elect. While people across the world, and indeed Jamaica, were celebrating this monumental victory, Bambino, along with two other men from the gang he rolled with, were at the Manchioneal beach in Portland awaiting the arrival of a go-fast boat from Haiti. They had 100 pounds of compressed marijuana to exchange for a bag of assorted weapons.

"Weh di bloodclaat boat deh so long man?" Bambino cursed impatiently to no one in particular. He hated waiting on anything. He checked the time. It was 11:50 p.m. He slapped his arm hard, killing the latest mosquito that had dared to steal some of his blood. He hurriedly relit his spliff, crouching and cupping his hands so as to keep the cool breeze from extinguishing the flame of his lighter.

He was the youngest of the three men present, but he was in charge. Matter of fact, although he was the youngest member of the entire gang, Birdman – so named for his hawk-like features, leader of the gang which controlled

Rosewater Meadows, treated him with the utmost respect and gave him a lot of leeway. Bambino answered to no one but Birdman.

Fifteen more minutes crept by before the boat finally arrived. Bambino sucked his teeth and the three men quickly unloaded the parcels of marijuana from the back of the pick-up truck and dumped them by the water's edge. The three men on the boat killed the engine and waded in the knee-high water to make the trade.

Bambino scowled at them as he took the bags with the guns from the outstretched arms of the tall, raggedly attired Haitian.

He checked the contents and didn't see three of the guns that he had expected to be there.

"What happen to de two Glock 45? And de Beretta?"

The tall Haitian shrugged his shoulders. "Dat is what we have man."

Bambino handed the bag of guns to one of the men from his gang and when the Haitians were loading the marijuana onto their boat, Bambino took back two of the twenty pound parcels.

"We nuh get all ah de gun dem…yuh caa get all ah de weed."

The Haitian scowled but didn't argue. He had heard about the trigger-happy youth who had killed twelve people by the age of sixteen. He was not somebody to get into an argument with. Especially not on his turf. He nodded curtly and joined his fellow country-men who had finished loading the rest of the parcels and were sitting in the boat waiting.

They then headed out quickly, anxious to get back to Port-Au-Prince. The boss would be upset that they only came back with sixty pounds of marijuana but it couldn't be helped.

Bambino reclined in the front seat of the Mitsubishi Sportero as they headed back to Kingston. He liked the new truck. It was one of three new vehicles that Birdman had procured for the gang over the past six months. Black, leather interior, powerful V12 engine, six disc CD changer, double cab; it was a good vehicle to make country runs in. The bag of guns and ammunition was in the back of the pick-up truck along with the two parcels of marijuana that Bambino had retained. They didn't even bother to conceal their illegal cargo as they planned to shoot it out with any cop that pulled them over and wanted to search the vehicle. They were well-armed and confident that they would get the better of any police patrol.

The ride to Kingston was uneventful, however, and an hour and a half after leaving the beach in Portland, they arrived in Kingston and headed straight to Rosewater Meadows.

Chapter 3

Birdman was in the backyard of his four bedroom house deep in the heart of Rosewater Meadows meeting with a few members of the gang when Bambino arrived. Birdman was in a foul mood. The police had set fire to forty acres of marijuana that a farmer in his employment had been growing in the hills of St. Elizabeth. It was a sizeable blow. He was depending on that crop to supply an order he had gotten from a guy in Miami. He wondered who had snitched to the cops. The farm had been very secluded. No way in hell the police had found it on their own.

"Bambino," he greeted. "What a gwaan?"

"Everyt'ing criss Birdman."

Bambino placed the bag of guns at his feet, and Danger, one of the guys who had also gone to Portland, did the same with the two parcels of marijuana.

Birdman looked at the marijuana in surprise. He arched his eyebrows at Bambino.

"De Haitian bwoy dem never supply all ah de gun dem...three was missing...so mi hold back forty pound ah de weed," he explained.

Birdman broke out in a wide grin. "Dats why mi haffi rate yuh enuh Bambino! Can always count pon yuh fi get de job done."

Birdman instructed two of the men to take everything inside and told Bambino to take a walk with him. They walked to the other side of the yard and stood by the short coconut tree.

They looked down into the gully which ran behind the yard. The gully separated Rosewater Meadows from Kirk Lane, another volatile community which was closely aligned with the rival political party of the one Rosewater Meadows supported. There had been some deadly clashes between the two communities over the years, especially, but not confined to, election time. A peace treaty had been signed six months ago but it was tenuous at best. Everyone knew that Birdman would not rest until Kirk Lane became a stronghold for the political party he supported. He was just biding his time.

Water was still flowing slowly through the gully from the heavy late evening rain. It was filthy and needed to be cleaned. Dead animals, condoms, clothing and other trash and debris decorated the murky moonlit water.

"Mi 'ave something personal mi need yuh fi deal wid fi mi," Birdman began.

Bambino waited for him to continue. His stomach was growling. He hadn't eaten since earlier the previous evening. It was now almost three in the morning.

"Dis youth over Spanish Town have some money ah siddung pon. Him contact mi de other day seh him want a car fi buy...cash. Mi tell 'im seh mi 'ave a nice 2005 Toyota Mark 11 can sell 'im fi six hundred thousand. So 'im come look pon it today. Him like it and supposed fi come wid de money fi buy it later this evening. Mi wah yuh fi go over 'im house and kill him and tek de money. If me do it when 'im come over here it ah go cause war because 'im affiliated with one ah de Spanish Town don dem. If wi mek it look like a robbery then our name caa call. One hundred thousand outta it would be yours."

Bambino lit a cigarette. A Newport. If he wasn't smoking weed, that's all he smoked.

"Alright, nuh problem. Two hundred mi want doah," he responded. None of the men in the gang if they were in his position would have asked for more money but he didn't fear Birdman. Matter of fact, there was nothing Bambino feared. A man who wasn't afraid to die, *expected* to die early, lived life without fear. He just *lived,* until his number was called.

Birdman chuckled. He had been around a long time but had never met anyone like Bambino. Only 18 years old, he had been a part of the gang for four years and was as fearless and coldhearted as they came. He wasn't exactly reckless. He just didn't give a shit. About anything at all. Except money. After growing up with nothing and going hungry more often than not, Bambino loved to look good and eat well. It cost money to be able to do that.

Birdman nodded.

He gave Bambino the man's address and told him to use a stolen car as he didn't want to take the chance of anyone seeing any of his vehicles in the vicinity.

Bambino told him that he would see him later.

He left the house on foot and walked for five minutes until he came to the home of a taxi driver that lived in the area. The man's car, a white Nissan Sentra that had seen better days, was parked outside the gate. Bambino touched the hood. It was still warm. Johnny, the taxi driver, had turned in for the night not too long ago.

He opened the zinc gate and went in, treating the dog who rushed over in the darkness to a hard kick to the mouth with his black Timberland boots. The dog howled in pain and ran away with its filthy tail tucked squarely between its legs.

There were two houses in the yard and he walked around to the second house where Johnny shared a room with his girlfriend, a thick mulatto from the country who was the chief recipient of most of the money Johnny earned on his daily route.

Bambino walked up to the bedroom window. Apparently Johnny was getting himself a bit of loving before going to sleep. The window was open. He climbed up on the two blocks that were under it and shifted the flimsy curtain to one side. Johnny's head was between his girlfriend's widely spread legs, having an early morning breakfast. She was moaning in ecstasy as Johnny noisily pleasured her with his mouth.

"Johnny!" Bambino shouted as he flicked his lighter and held it in the room.

Johnny jumped up in fright and fell off the bed as the young woman, apparently frozen in surprise, did not move.

"Jesus Christ! Bambino! Yuh ah try fi gi mi heart attack?" Johnny said as he rose from the floor, his face red with embarrassment at what he had been caught doing. It was taboo in the ghetto to perform cunnilingus.

"Put on yuh clothes. Mi need yuh fi carry mi somewhere. Now. And brush yuh fucking teeth," Bambino told him and stepped away from the window.

Johnny quickly did as he was told. It wouldn't do to get on Bambino's wrong side. His girlfriend watched him silently as he hurriedly dressed and brushed his teeth. Johnny was such a punk. She had met him six months ago when she first arrived in Kingston to stay with her cousin in Rosewater Meadows. Life in the country was too boring and slow. She was young and sexy. She wanted to be able to have fun and party all the time. She had taken Johnny's taxi to her cousin's home and taking a liking to her, he had not charged her any fare. She had given him her number and he had paid her numerous visits, bringing lunch for her during the days and dinner at night when she wanted it, which she always did. She had moved in with him after two months, and though she knew she wouldn't be for him for very long, he treated her very well so she decided to take advantage of it until something better came her way.

A lot of men in the community were after her, but she hadn't seen the right one yet. A couple of them looked really cute and could dress, especially one who was a popular dancer, but she was all about money. They had nothing to offer her. The guy that had Johnny acting like a frightened bitch was more her speed. A gangster that was getting money. He was hot too. A bit on the skinny side but cute with his straight nose and curly hair. She had seen him passing by the corner where she often hung out with her cousin and her friends on many occasions. He was usually in a nice vehicle with the don of the community or other members of the gang. Bambino. She had asked her cousin about him. Her cousin had told her that Bambino was a bad man that only cared about killing people. He didn't want anybody. He might fuck her once, like he did a lot of the hot girls in the community – including her – but he wouldn't stick around and he didn't give women money. She also said with a raucous laugh that Bambino had the biggest dick she had ever seen. That hadn't turned off Deidre one bit. She was intrigued by the quiet, gangster youth that was only a year older than her.

"Later Deidre," Johnny said as he hurried through the door.

Bambino was waiting for him beside the car.

He climbed into the backseat and Johnny headed out.

"So weh we ah go?" Johnny queried, careful to keep his tone light as he glanced at Bambino through the rearview mirror.

"Twin Gates plaza," was the reply.

There was a 24 hour fast food joint there and Bambino needed to eat before he went on this mission. He didn't like distractions and being this hungry was definitely a distraction.

The streets were empty save for a few homeless people and a couple of cars zipping by. They got to Half-Way-Tree quickly and Johnny pulled up inside the Twin Gates parking lot. There were several cars in front of the fast food joint. Bambino wasn't the only one hungry at this time of the morning. He handed Johnny a thousand dollar bill.

"Get me a number 2," he instructed.

Johnny switched off the engine and went to do Bambino's bidding.

He cursed to himself as he waited in line. He had a son older than Bambino. Yet if Bambino told him jump, there would immediately be air beneath his feet. Life was fucked up at times. But that's the way it goes. You have to take the good with the bad. It was guys like Bambino who kept the neighbourhood safe from predators from rival communities who would have come in and have their way had there not been a strong gang to maintain the order. Birdman and the gang had their faults – he didn't agree with the way they dealt with things sometimes – but he had to admit that it was the safest the community had ever been from rival gunmen.

"You had to catch, kill an' cook de fucking chicken?" Bambino asked sarcastically when Johnny returned with the food fifteen minutes later.

"In deh did pack man," Johnny replied.

Bambino, with the door open, sat on the backseat and ate his food quickly.

The barbecue chicken, pumpkin rice and festival was good, but even if it wasn't, he was too hungry to notice, or care.

Johnny wanted to ask what was next as he anxiously wanted to get back home. The thought of Deidre lying in the bed naked waiting for him was driving him crazy. He could still taste her sweet pussy on his tongue, though he had brushed his teeth. He hoped Bambino wouldn't tell anyone that he had seen him going down on Deidre. He would be the laughing stock at the taxi stand. He knew a lot of them did it and pretended otherwise but it was another thing to be actually caught in action. Bambino was a quiet guy though and wasn't known to engage in idle chatter so maybe, just maybe, he wouldn't say anything to anyone.

Bambino gulped his grape soda down and uttered a loud belch.

A stickler for cleanliness, he placed the empty containers in the bag and told Johnny to dump it in the trash container that was inside the restaurant. When Johnny came back out, Bambino was gone. A five hundred dollar bill was on the driver's seat.

Bambino watched as Johnny looked around alarmed, then relieved when he saw the money on the seat. He had thought that Bambino had left without paying him. He then turned his attention back to the trembling lady who was staring straight ahead and holding the steering wheel tightly with both hands, as he had instructed. They were in the same parking lot as Johnny, who was now driving out, just two cars down from where Johnny had parked.

Bambino had noticed a young woman, dressed in sweats, flip flops and a tank top, walking briskly towards them just as he gave Johnny the trash to dispose of. He had quickly exited the car and pulling his desert eagle from his waist, had slid into the passenger side of her blue Honda Accord just as she got in and was about to close the door. The scream had died in her throat when she saw the gun. He had told her to keep quiet, look straight ahead and place her hands on the steering wheel.

Bambino looked at the young woman. She was in her mid-twenties, attractive though she had bad skin, and shivering with fear.

"Leave de parking lot using the Eastwood Park Road exit," he instructed.

The young woman was crying silently. She drove out slowly and reluctantly as though she was afraid that if she left the parking lot she would be heading towards her death. As soon as they got to the other side of the large parking lot, just a few meters from the exit to Eastwood Park road, Bambino told her to stop the car.

She did and turned to look at him fearfully.

Bambino was sure that he had told her to look straight ahead. He hated when people couldn't follow simple instructions. Anyhow, it didn't matter at this juncture.

"Come out ah de car and come around to my side...walk in front ah de car," he told her.

She took a deep breath and did as she was told.

Bambino came out of the car and gave her a single shot to the heart. She died instantly. He noticed a very nice diamond ring on her right index finger. Would be a shame to waste such a nice piece of jewellery. He slipped it off and placed it in his pocket.

He then hopped in and drove out without as much as a cursory glance around to see if he had been observed. He turned left at the Dunrobin stoplight and headed out to Spanish Town. He had nothing against the young lady. He simply needed her car and didn't want to have to deal with the hassle if he had let her go and she had managed to call the cops.

Collateral damage.

She had just been in the wrong place at the wrong time. He looked over at the large bag filled with food on the backseat that the young lady had purchased. Whoever was waiting on some of that food had a very long wait. He reached into the bag and pulled out some fries without taking his eye off the road. He ate a lot. People always wondered where his food went as he never seemed to gain any weight despite his voracious appetite.

If they ever saw him naked, they would know exactly where his food went.

Chapter 4

Bambino got to Spanish Town in half an hour. The strip club on the Brunswick was still open though it was obvious that nothing was going on inside. All the strippers were standing outside on the balcony. He glanced over there and recognized a black Mercedes sedan that was parked in front of the club. Good thing his windows were tinted. The owner of the car was an enemy of Birdman's. If he saw Bambino over here at this time of the morning, when news broke of the murder he was about to commit, there was no doubt that his name would be called. He drove quickly, making the right turn in front of the Pet Com gas station. He then took the first left, and then the second right; and drove pass his target's house at Lot 16. He made a U-turn and parked the vehicle in front of Lot 15. He got out and walked over to Lot 16. He jumped the wall easily. A man and his elderly mother occupied the right side of the house while Rhino, his target, lived with his baby mother and two children on the left.

Bambino walked to the back of the house. There were two separate back doors leading to the two dwellings. He tried his trusty lock opener in both doors. They wouldn't budge. He then checked the kitchen window on the left side. The bottom ones were closed but the top was open. He looked around for something to stand on. He was tall – six feet – but didn't want to stretch and risk one falling and breaking. He found a crate and stood on it. He deftly removed the windows and placed them carefully on the ground. He then entered the house.

He frowned at the pile of dirty dishes in the kitchen sink, visible from the moonlight filtering through the open window. *Rhino's girl must be one nasty bitch to go bed leaving the kitchen in such a deplorable state.* He pulled his gun and entered the living room. It was much darker in there. He moved carefully as headed to the bedrooms. He figured the adults would have the room closest to the front. He opened the door slowly and went in. He was correct. He could make out the two figures in the bed. Rhino was on the left, lying on his side. He was snoring heavily.

Bambino walked over to him and shoved the gun inside his open mouth. He palmed the back of Rhino's head, helping him up as he woke up disoriented.

"Yuh nah dream pussy, yuh really 'ave a gun inna yuh stinking mouth," Bambino said softly.

Rhino's eyes were wide as he fully awakened and realized what was happening.

"Weh de money deh?" Bambino asked.

Rhino didn't hesitate. He pointed downwards with a trembling finger.

"Under de bed?"

He shook his head in the affirmative.

Bambino removed the gun from his mouth.

"Get it," he instructed.

Rhino got down on his knees and reached under the bed. He pulled out a large duffel bag.

Rhino's girlfriend changed positions on the bed but did not awaken.

"Carry de bag out to de living room," Bambino told him. Rhino shuffled out with the bag, too scared to be concerned about his nudity.

Bambino followed closely behind him with the gun trained on the back of his head. He pulled the door shut as he exited the bedroom.

"Turn on de light and lie down pon yuh belly wid yuh hand dem by yuh side," Bambino growled.

Rhino did as he told, grimacing as he lay awkwardly on his exposed genitals. But he dared not move his hands lest his tormentor thought he was trying something. The floor felt cold on his bare skin.

There was something familiar about the youth but he couldn't place it. He wondered who had sent him. A few people knew that he had the money in the house but none of them would dare pull a stunt like this. Everyone knew that he was affiliated with Peanuts, one of the top dons in Spanish Town. So who was this youth? A random robber? He didn't think so.

Bambino looked in the bag and smiled.

The money was there all right.

But there were also two parcels of a white substance in the bag.

Cocaine.

A welcome bonus.

He zipped the bag shut and slung it over his shoulder.

It was time to go.

Rhino was still trying to figure out who had sent the robber when Bambino shot him in the head, splattering the contents of his brain all over the terrazzo tiles.

He let himself out through the front door, moving with measured haste. He could hear Rhino's girl calling his name when she turned on the bedroom light and didn't see him. He jumped the wall and entered the car. He could hear her screams as he gunned the engine and drove away.

Rhino had not uttered one word the entire time.

He hadn't even begged for his life, though it was obvious that he had been scared shitless.

Bambino respected that.

Rhino had died like a man.

Chapter 5

Christine received the call while she was in the shower getting ready for work. Her phone had rung loudly and insistently from its perch on the toilet. She had turned the shower off, dried her hands and answered the call.

It was her sister's best friend, Lorraine.

She had been sobbing and was so incoherent that it had taken Christine a full five minutes before she could understand what Lorraine was saying.

Her sister was dead.

Murdered early this morning in the Twin Gates parking lot.

She had uttered a piercing cry that had sent her house-mate and best friend Miranda, who was already dressed for work and was in her bedroom applying the finishing touches to her make-up, scurrying to the bathroom in fright.

Christine was inconsolable. She and her older sister had been very close. Most of the family lived abroad, including their mother, who after divorcing their father seven years ago, had migrated to England. Their father had passed away from cardiac arrest a few months after his wife had left him for another man. The girls had blamed their mother for his death. They were convinced that the stress of dealing with losing his wife in such an unexpected and heartbreaking manner; had sent him to an early grave. Their relationship with their mother had been very strained over the years to say the least.

Miranda cried as she hugged Christine tightly.

Her work clothes were now wet and crushed.

But it didn't matter.

Neither of them made it to work that day.

Bambino woke up at 2 p.m. He had slept all day after getting back to Rosewater Meadows at six in the morning. He was home at the house he lived in for free. As a political activist, his name had been on the list to receive one of the low income houses that the government had built in Rosewater Meadows as part of their inner-city development program. The one bedroom home was very clean and well-kept. It was sparsely but expensively furnished: a plush black leather couch set; a 36 inch flat screen T.V.; a thick bold red Chinese rug; a queen-sized bed that practically took up all of the space in the bedroom and a large aluminum refrigerator that dominated the small kitchen. An elderly woman that had been one of the few people to extend any sort of kindness to him when he was growing up, cleaned his home twice a week for ten thousand dollars a month. He checked his mobile which he had placed on vibrate so as not to disturb him. He had missed ten calls. Two were from Birdman. Bambino yawned, stretched and returned the call as he made his way to the kitchen. There was some leftover food in the fridge. He placed it in the microwave and went into the living room and turned on the T.V. He turned to the soccer channel as Birdman picked up.

"Yo Bambino...everyt'ing criss?" he asked, alluding to the robbery.

"Yeah, mi soon come check yuh," Bambino told him.

"Alright, mi deh home so link mi."

Bambino hung up as he checked out the scores in the English Premier League from over the weekend. He had been busy on the street and hadn't gotten a chance to watch the matches over the weekend. He nodded his approval when he saw that Liverpool had beaten Arsenal. This year might be the year that they finally break their championship drought. They hadn't won a league title since he had been born. He loved them though; there was something about the team that made him an ardent fan.

He heard the microwave beep and he went to fetch his food. He dug into the stew chicken and dumplings he had bought two days ago but hadn't eaten as he planned the rest of his day.

After swinging by Birdman to give him his share of the money, he would go uptown to check a drug dealer that he knew. He didn't want to sell the cocaine to anyone who knew Birdman. It would raise questions about where he had gotten the coke and why he hadn't notified Birdman about it. There was also a weekly Wednesday night dance on Burlington Avenue that he felt as though he would attend tonight. He would get a new outfit at the mall later. He deserved to have some fun. The last few days had been very productive. He finished his food and went to take a shower.

Christine was back home at her apartment after completing the heartbreaking task of identifying her sister's body. She was not alone. Lorraine, her sister's best friend, and Miranda, her housemate, were there with her. Her boyfriend, Clive, was in Antigua on business and wouldn't be able to come back to Jamaica before Friday.

Going to the morgue to identify her sister's body was one of the hardest things Christine had ever done in her twenty four years. Her eyes were puffy and swollen. She had been crying nonstop since she had gotten the horrible news. Her boss at the commercial bank where she worked as a personal banking assistant; had given her two weeks leave.

"Oh God! Why poor Nadine had to die? Jesus Christ! Why yuh tek mi sister before her time?" Christine wailed in anguish.

No one answered. What could they say?

Mercifully, Christine fell asleep after a little while from sheer stress and exhaustion.

"Yuh tek out your cut?" Birdman said to Bambino, more of an observation than a question. They were in Birdman's bedroom, away from the prying eyes of some of the gang members who were at the house, as well as Queenie, Birdman's longtime girlfriend. He was a bit peeved that Bambino hadn't brought him everything and allowed him to give him his cut. Sometimes Bambino's own way attitude really grated on his nerves. But Bambino was his best and most trusted soldier. He needed him. For now.

"Yeah," Bambino replied nonchalantly. He knew that Birdman didn't like the fact that he couldn't fully control him. He didn't care. Though he respected Birdman, he was his own man when it came down to it. And that was that.

"So 'im never 'ave nothin' else inna de house?" Birdman asked, his narrow eyes watching Bambino's reaction closely.

He had heard that the guy, Rhino, handled some of the drugs that Peanuts sold.

"No sah...just the cash," Bambino responded easily.

Birdman didn't see any signs that suggested that Bambino was lying. But that didn't mean he wasn't. His source that told him about the drugs was reliable. He found it a bit strange that there wasn't any in the house at all. Did Bambino really have the balls to cross him like that? The answer was an emphatic yes but he didn't think he would. Bambino had never crossed him before. Why would he start now?

They each had a beer and a spliff as they discussed some moves to be made in the coming days. Birdman commended Bambino on leaving the stolen car close to the entrance of Kirk Lane. That would bring some heat from the cops to the rival community.

Smart move.

Half an hour later, Bambino told Birdman that he was going on the road and that he would see him later when it was time to link up and go to the party. Birdman had agreed to go as well when Bambino had mentioned that he would be going to the party later.

Bambino hopped on to his black and chrome CBR 1000 motorbike, which he had ridden to go and see Birdman, and headed uptown. The bike had been one of a number of items seized by the police at the home of a drug dealer who was extradited to the US eight months ago. One of the cops in the special task force that had apprehended the drug dealer was someone that Birdman did business with from time to time. Bambino had fallen in love with the powerful motorbike and after a lengthy negotiation the cop had sold him the bike for only a fraction of its true value. The parcels of cocaine were in a Louis Vuitton backpack on his back. He knew that Birdman wouldn't have given the bag a second glance as he knew that it was a current style.

Bambino loved to ride. Riding suited his free flowing, fast paced lifestyle and personality in a way that a vehicle never could.

He weaved through the heavy traffic skillfully as he headed up Constant Spring road. He got to the guy's apartment, located in a gated complex, in ten minutes.

The guy, a half-Chinese, twenty-five year old named Randy, was entertaining. There were two girls there that Bambino was sure weren't a day over fifteen.

Not his concern.

They went into a bedroom that doubled as an office and got down to business.

The guy measured the cocaine on his triple beam scale.

Twenty ounces of raw cocaine.

A street value of USD$65000.

"I can't pay you what it's really worth," Randy said to Bambino. "There's a recession going on in the States which is my primary market. Nothing is immune. Not even drugs."

Bambino thought about the situation. The cocaine was raw and it was high quality. That meant it could be cut several times without the quality being adversely affected. The profit would be substantial. But he wasn't a drug dealer. And he needed to get rid of the cocaine quickly. Besides it was free money.

"Mek me an offer," he responded.

"I can give you USD$10,000 in cash right now and take it off your hands," Randy said. They both knew that it was a rip off but they both also knew that Bambino wouldn't have come all the way uptown if he hadn't wanted certain people not to know about this deal.

"Give me twelve and gwaan wid it," Bambino countered.

"Eleven thousand...final offer," Randy replied.

Bambino did the math in his head. With an exchange rate of 77 to 1 he would get almost eight hundred and fifty thousand Jamaican dollars. Not bad but it was a pity he couldn't get a clear million.

"Alright, deal."

They shook hands and the guy went into the other room and returned with the money. Eleven stacks of ten one hundred dollar bills. Bambino counted the money and placed it in his backpack.

"Great doing business with you Bambino," Randy said.

"Yuh get a sweet bloodclaat deal today...best yuh might ever get inna yuh life. Yuh owe me a favour. Might call it in one ah dese days," Bambino said, looking at him steadily. Randy was a good person to know. He had all kinds of contacts.

Randy laughed and told him no problem.

Bambino glanced at the two girls as he walked through the living room. They were kissing.

Chapter 6

"Lighter inna de air!" the disc jockey shouted in the microphone as he played one of the hottest songs currently raging in the dancehall. The crowd voiced their approval by shouting and firing blanks in the air with their hands. More than a few flashed their lighters in cooperation with the disc jockey's request and the excitement was fever pitch where the artist, who was the proud owner of the song, was standing with his entourage in the unofficial VIP section of the venue.

Bambino, Birdman, and ten members of their gang were also in that section.

There was tension in the air.

The artist, called Tech Nyne, was from Kirk Lane and though there was a truce between Kirk Lane and Rosewater Meadows, everyone knew that the slightest thing, even a *perceived* slight, could trigger something off. The men from Kirk Lane seemed to be rubbing the success of their hometown hero in the faces of the men from Rosewater Meadows. Champagne was being sprayed and comments were being made. They were thoroughly enjoying the moment.

Bambino just wanted a drop of the champagne that they were spraying around to even touch his brand new crispy blue and white high-top Air Force ones. Their celebration would be over in a split second. Nothing happened though, and the rowdy bunch calmed down a bit when the disc jockey changed the pace and started playing some R&B. Neyo's *Independent Woman* had the girls going wild.

Bambino watched as Deidre moved her waistline like a seasoned exotic dancer. She was wearing a short black dress that did little to hide the lush package that it was supposed to be covering. She pulled it down constantly as she gyrated seductively. She was with a group of eight girls, all dressed in skimpy outfits and dancing like they were performing at a strip club on a Friday night when every man in the venue had just gotten paid. She knew he was watching. She had turned around to face where he was standing a few times while she was performing her seductive moves. Bambino remembered when he had seen her sprawled out in the bed, moaning under Johnny's oral attention.

His dick stirred in the close confines of his fitted Rock Republic jeans.

He sipped his glass of champagne.

He was going to fuck her tonight.

He sent one of the gang members to tell her to meet him in the VIP parking lot after the party was the over.

The guy frowned inwardly but went to do his bidding.

The smile that appeared on Deidre's face when she got the message was bright enough to light up the party.

Johnny was parked outside the venue waiting for Deidre and her friends. He had dropped them there earlier and was back to take them home. He was feeling particularly good. Today was his birthday. He had turned forty-four three hours ago. He was going to go home and have a great time with Deidre in bed. He knew she had been drinking and gyrating all night. She would be extremely horny. He couldn't wait. He continued to laugh and chat with two of his friends who were there trying to find passengers to take home.

"Dah young gal deh ah go kill yuh," one of them was saying to Johnny, much to the amusement of the other guy. "Yuh caa manage dat...de gal thick an' fit like fiddle."

Johnny merely laughed. They were just envious. He had a hot, young, sexy filly that both of them would kill to have at home as opposed to the miserable, over the hill, wrinkled companions they were stuck with.

A few minutes later, Banga, the one with the exceptionally large stomach, excitedly said to Johnny, "But wait! Nuh yuh woman dat ah go over deh so with de gangster dem?"

His heart suddenly in a tight knot, Johnny looked where Banga was pointing.

He could make out Deidre, along with two of her friends, walking in the midst of the gang from Rosewater Meadows.

Hearing but not listening to the merciless teasing by his friends, Johnny watched slack-jawed as the entourage quickly exited the parking lot in their caravan of luxury vehicles. He saw Deidre on the back of Bambino's bike, her voluptuous ass perched sexily in the air as she lowered her head and held Bambino around the waist.

Johhny's face became a curious shade of purple and red as embarrassment and anger fought for control of his features. If someone had cut him with a knife right then and there, there would not have been a drop of blood.

"We ready Johnny," one of Deidre's friends whom he had given a lift earlier declared as she smacked the gum she was chewing. She was standing by the car along with the other four girls who apparently had not been 'chosen' to hang with the gangsters tonight.

She visibly recoiled from Johnny when she saw the look that he gave her.

"But ah weh yuh ah look pon mi so fah Johnny? Yuh t'ink seh ah my fault yuh woman gone fuck ah next man?"

Johnny lost it.

He attacked the young woman with a barrage of hard punches to the face and body. Her friends, after their initial shock, jumped on him and one of them removed a knife from her pocketbook and used it to stab Johnny repeatedly in the back and side. By the time the cops came, the girls had been whisked away by a friend of theirs from Rosewater Meadows and Johnny was on the ground bleeding profusely from multiple stab wounds. The cops allowed his friends to take him to the hospital, promising to come and see him for questioning in a little while. They questioned some of the people that were still milling around the scene about what had happened. All they received were stony stares and insults from some of the braver souls.

No one gave them any information.

Deidre was very impressed when she entered Bambino's house. It was small like most of the ones in this section of Rosewater Meadows, except for the few that the owners had added on to, but inside, she was positive that none could compare. She felt like she was in an expensive hotel suite. She followed Bambino to the bedroom slowly as she looked around.

Bambino had not uttered a single word to her all night. She thought it was best to follow suit. He turned on the light and she watched as he removed the large handgun from his waist and placed it on a tiny table that was against the wall. He then started to take off his clothes. She followed his lead.

He finished undressing before her and climbed onto the massive bed. He reclined against two large, fluffy pillows and watched her with a stoic expression.

Deidre stood with her dress in her hand.

Her mouth was a wide O.

Her eyes were even wider.

They were riveted on his dick.

It looked almost bigger than he was.

It was beyond her comprehension how a man with such a skinny frame could manage to walk around with such an enormous appendage.

Her cousin had not exaggerated in the least.

He was already aroused.

His dick was waving like an iron flag.

She wondered if she could take all of it.

There was no way she could.

She knew she had no choice.

She dropped her dress on the carpeted floor and removed her thong.

She joined Bambino on the bed.

She felt lightheaded.

She was nervous, anxious, scared and horny all at the same time.

"Suck it," Bambino said, uttering his first words to her.

Though Johnny would never know, she was very good at giving fellatio. A white businessman that she had met in Negril when she went on a beach trip several years ago had taken her virginity and taught her everything that she knew about sex. He had been a very freaky man and she had indulged him, loving the gifts and money she would receive whenever she spent time with him. She had only been fourteen years old at the time but had the body of a twenty year old woman. She never heard from him again after he went back to Europe at the end of his month long business trip.

Bambino was silent when her warm mouth enveloped the head of his turgid dick though it felt really good. He watched her as she tried to see how much of it she could take in her mouth.

Not much.

She concentrated on running her lips along the sides of his shaft and licking and sucking the bulbous head. She finally elicited a low moan from Bambino when she took his scrotum in her mouth and wrapped her tongue around his heavy testicles.

Then it was time for the moment of truth.

Bambino wordlessly gave her a condom.

She removed it from the wrapper and her hands shook mightily as she rolled it onto his dick.

He didn't move so she got on top of him and positioned herself high over his member, using her right hand to guide it to the entrance of her willing but deathly afraid orifice.

She made an unintelligible sound when it pierced her. Her breathing ragged, she moved slowly downwards, stopping after just a few inches, and bounced on the head, as she tried to acclimatize herself to his massive tool.

She was grateful that Bambino, at least for now, was relaxing and letting her dictate the pace. She already felt it in her stomach and she hadn't even taken half of it yet.

"Bloodclaat...Bambino...ohhh...oww...oh God...ohhh ..."

She soon got into a rhythm and her ass cheeks were a blur as she bounced rapidly on the head.

Bambino joined the ranks of the white man who had taken her virginity as the only men to make her climax from penetration as she held her head skyward and flooded his dick with her juices.

"Bambino! Bambino! Bumboclaat! Bumboclaat!" she blasphemed as she shook violently, her face contorted in an intricate mix of pain and ecstasy. He hadn't even done anything. He had just laid there and yet she had climaxed quickly. And hard. She could only imagine what it was going to be like when he *really* started to put it on her. She didn't have long to wait.

Bambino flipped her like a pancake and threw her thick legs on his bony shoulders.

He gave her all of it.

Long, deep, measured strokes.

Deidre's cries of agony and pleasure could be heard eight houses away.

Chapter 7

A month later, Christine was sitting by the window facing the street having lunch with her co-worker when she noticed the pretty black and chrome motorbike that had pulled up outside of the popular fast food restaurant. The rider parked the bike and kicked down the stand but did not disembark. He sat there for a few minutes and she watched as a car pulled up behind it. The driver got out and conversed with the man sitting on the bike. The man seemed to be pleading his case about something. The rider appeared to be unmoved. He was looking at the man with a bored expression.

"Who yuh looking at…that cute guy on the bike?" her lunch companion, Colette, asked through a mouthful of fries.

Christine smiled. She didn't respond as she continued to stare at the young man. He was more pretty than handsome. His curly, unruly mane; deep expressionless eyes; straight nose and high cheekbones were very easy on the eyes. Almost too pretty for a man but his tough guy aura balanced out the equation well.

Though he seemed relaxed sitting on top of the motorcycle, Christine got the impression that he was like a coiled cobra, capable of springing on an unsuspecting prey at any given time.

She was so right.

She gasped as he slapped the other man on the mouth.

The man was clearly embarrassed but did not retaliate.

He merely continued to plead.

The pretty man said something to the other guy as he restarted his motorbike.

He then rode off.

Christine was shocked and intrigued by what she had just seen.

Who the hell was that guy?

Bambino stopped at the gas station across from the police post in New Kingston to fill up his tank. He was armed and was wanted for questioning in a number of incidents across the corporate area but he had no apprehensions about going around freely. If they approached him on a bad day, it would be a shootout. If he was in a good mood, he might speak to them and allow them to take him in. He would be out in no time anyway. If one of the gang's contacts in the force couldn't spring him, then the prominent lawyer that represented Birdman and his gang any time they had legal issues, would get him out.

He was mildly annoyed.

Someone was supposed to have provided him with some information regarding a warehouse owned by a Chinese businessman that was said to be housing one thousand pounds of compressed ganja for export to the United Kingdom. It was a massive shipment. Bambino wanted to rob the warehouse before they managed to get the marijuana out of the country. But he didn't know where in Kingston the warehouse was located and his source that was to have provided the information today had come up short. Bambino suspected that he had gotten cold feet. All of a sudden he claimed he couldn't find out exactly where the warehouse was located. Bambino had let him off with a slap and a warning that he had better come up with the information by tomorrow.

He saw Johnny's taxi drive by as he gunned his engine and turned down Knutsford Boulevard. He chuckled to himself. Johnny had spent a week in the hospital after being stabbed by Deidre's friend. And after he came out, he had gone straight to Deidre's cousin's home and begged Deidre to come back home with him. After a few days of groveling, Deidre had gone back to stay with him. Johnny was the laughing stock of the community but he didn't care. He loved Deidre and he couldn't live without her.

Bambino had fucked Deidre twice since their first encounter. It was a long time since he had enjoyed having sex with someone more than once. There was something about the way she fucked him that stirred his soul. She was an animal in bed and he liked that. It had taken her a few days before she was able to walk normally after that first time and though she had figured that she would get use to his size over time, it was the same result the other times they copulated. Bambino was just too large.

She had confessed to him that she no longer allowed Johnny to penetrate her. It wouldn't make any sense. She only allowed him to give her oral sex now. Bambino had laughed. He wondered what men like Johnny were made of. He would rather be dead than live like that.

His thoughts drifted back to the marijuana issue as he waited for the stoplight to change at Cross Roads. If the man didn't come through with the info, he would tell Birdman to let them simply kidnap the Chinese business-man and make him give up the information in exchange for his life.

But one way or another, he was going to get that weed.

"No...Clive...stop..." Christine protested as her boyfriend of three years started kissing her on the neck. They had not had sex since her sister's murder. She knew he was frustrated but she just wasn't in the mood. Her usually healthy libido had taken a nose dive.

She was slowly coming to terms with losing her sister but she needed a bit more time before she completely got back to her normal, vibrant self. The lead detective on the case, who she figured was making an extra effort because he liked her, had called to say that the gun used to kill her sister was used in a murder in Spanish Town a few hours later. The shell casings at both crime scenes were the same. He surmised that her car had been used as transportation to commit the murder in Spanish Town before being driven back to Kingston and dumped in the ghetto of Kirk Lane. He didn't think the killer was from Kirk Lane though. He figured that was just a ploy but he had taken in some people for questioning anyway.

She had thanked him for the information though she didn't give a shit about the details. She just wanted to hear him say that they had found her sister's murderer.

"Christine...how long are things going to be like this?" Clive asked in annoyance, breaking into her thoughts. He removed his arm from around her. "What do you expect me to do in the meantime?"

Christine looked at him wearily. She used to think that he was such a considerate person, so loving and under-standing. He was disappointing her. He *knew* how devastated she was over Nadine's murder. She had had to go on medication after the funeral. She couldn't sleep and she wasn't eating. The medication was working though and she was doing much better now but still had some ways to go. Yet here he was. Stressing her out for sex. Why couldn't he understand?

"Gee I don't know Clive, what do you want me to tell you? That you should go and fuck somebody else until I'm ready? Or better yet...that you should get some lube and lubricate my dry vagina and fuck me until you're satisfied?"

Clive's left eye always twitched uncontrollably when he was furious.

It was twitching now.

"That's not fair Christine! How can you say that? All I'm saying is that you have to understand that this is affecting me too! I still have my needs. I've been there by your side...supporting you...helping out anyway I can...but what about me? I have a right to ask how long it's going to be like this. Rass man! Be reasonable! It's been a little over a month Christine!"

"You know what Clive...if you really think I need this shit right now, something's wrong with you. I think you should go...I don't want to fight with you."

Clive sighed in frustration.

He just wasn't getting through to her.

She just couldn't put herself in his shoes for a second and try to see where he was coming from.

He got up and left without another word.

The apartment vibrated from the force at which he slammed the door.

Christine sighed and turned up the volume on the T.V. Clive was acting like a horny 18 year old that couldn't think straight instead of a 30 year old man. If he had a grouse, that was not the way to come at her. Not now. He had better get his act together. He knew that she wasn't one for the bullshit. She curled up comfortably on the couch and tried to focus on the Michelle Obama interview on CBS. She was going to follow the doctor's advice and avoid stressful situations. If Clive continued like this, they just might have to take a break from each other.

Miranda had been in her room reading when she heard them arguing. It was one of those situations where neither party was wrong. She understood that Christine was still healing, and she also understood that Clive had his needs as a man. He probably shouldn't have expressed himself in anger though. He knew his girl. That approach would get him nowhere. Though Christine was out there alone, Miranda stayed put. Most likely Christine would want to be by herself. She hoped the argument didn't escalate further though. They were a nice couple. Clive was a good guy. He looked ok if not cute, had a nice, well-paying job and he treated Christine well. He was also a very good lover if Christine's cries of passion whenever she heard them having sex was anything to go by. She raised her eyebrows. There was an unexpected development in the novel she was reading. It was really heating up now.

Chapter 8

Peanuts was grim as he got off phone with his police contact at the Spanish Town police station. He now knew who had killed and robbed Rhino. He had suspected Birdman when he had heard about it as he knew that Rhino, despite being warned not to do any business with Birdman, had gone to visit him regarding the purchase of a car. No one from Spanish Town would have dared to rob someone affiliated with him so he had deduced that Birdman, knowing that Rhino had a lot of cash in his house, had decided to rob him. The thing he was most upset about though, aside from the disrespect, was that they also took his cocaine. Twenty eight ounces. There was no way he was going to let that slide.

"Ah Birdman dem kill Rhino fi real," he said to Wayne, his right-hand man. They were in the back room of his restaurant and bar on Brunswick Avenue.

"How yuh so sure?" Wayne queried.

"Mi police brethren seh 'im hear seh de same gun weh kill ah gal ah Kingston de same mornin' Rhino dead, ah de same gun weh use fi kill Rhino. Plus dem find de dead gal car over Kirk Lane. Yuh know seh ah somebody put it dere fi mek it look like seh is a man from Kirk Lane do de killings."

Wayne tugged on the end of one of his long cornrows in concentration. What Peanuts said made perfect sense. He nodded his head in agreement.

"Yeah man," Peanuts continued, "pussyhole dem tek mi coke. Mi want it back, plus interest. If ah war dem want, ah war dem ah go bloodclaat get. But first, mi ah go give dem a chance fi mek t'ings right. Mi ah go call de bwoy Birdman."

Wayne nodded again. It was best to avoid an all out conflict if possible. Too much gun play was bad for business. Hopefully Birdman would settle this like a man and repay what he took. A life for Rhino's life, the money and the cocaine, plus interest as a token of future goodwill. He wouldn't hold his breath though. Birdman was a knucklehead. Most likely they would have to do this the hard way.

He said as much to Peanuts.

Peanuts agreed but said he would still try. He was from the old school. He wasn't as trigger-happy as these gangsters nowadays. But when it came down to it, he could be as ruthless as ever. He had been the don for his section of Spanish Town for twenty years. You didn't stay on top that long without being smart and having the right team around you. Wayne was young but wise beyond his years. He would be ready to take over if anything should ever happen to him.

He would call Birdman a little later.

It was almost time to have his dinner and he didn't want to upset his stomach.

Bambino was unable to get through to the man who was supposed to furnish the information regarding the warehouse housing the large quantity of marijuana. His phone was off. He and Birdman then worked out the logistics for plan B: kidnapping the Chinese businessman. They headed to Half-Way-Tree where the head office for his furniture chain was located. He was there now. They had someone call and ask to speak with him and the caller had been told that he was in a meeting. They used two vehicles, the Mitsubishi Sportero and a Mitsubishi Evolution IV. Bambino, not being able to ride his bike on this mission, was driving the Evolution which was the next best thing. It was super fast. Danger was riding with him while two others were in the truck with Birdman.

They got to the office complex and parked across the road at a small plaza which housed a sports bar upstairs. They went up there to knock back a few rounds while they waited. The man would be leaving his office at 6 p.m. to play squash at a private business club in New Kingston. That gave them forty-five minutes to kill. The two women that would be taking part in the mission were on their way.

Three Guiness Stouts and a game of pool later, it was time. They filed out and made their way to the vehicles. They got in and waited for the drama to unfold.

The girl, Birdman's girlfriend's younger sister, had just arrived. She pulled over on the side of the road directly in front of the office complex. She got out of the car, a red Honda Civic coupe, and opened the hood.

The Chinese businessman exited the complex in his pearl white Mercedes SUV and slowed down as he approached the woman peering helplessly into the engine. She was professionally attired in a black skirt suit with stockings and black pumps; however, he thought her skirt was way too tight. None of his employees could dress so provocatively to work but she wasn't his employee now was she? She had a very sexy body. He stopped and admired her plump derriere for a few seconds before he spoke.

"Hello, everything ok?"

Nisha turned her head.

"No...my car won't start," she told him, looking distressed. She straightened up and turned around.

His slanted eyes roamed from her cute brown face to her firm mouthwatering breasts straining against her top and back.

"Well I'm no mechanic but I'll call one to come and have a look," he told her as he took out his Blackberry Bold.

"Thank you..." Nisha said, smiling sweetly.

"No problem sexy." He smiled magnanimously as he dialed.

Queenie, Birdman's girlfriend and Nisha's older half-sister, appeared from around the corner where Nisha had dropped her off, and walked towards the vehicle pretending to be preoccupied with her phone.

"Yeah, right in front of my office complex," the Chinese businessman was saying, his eyes on the bit of cleavage Nisha was displaying. She was now standing directly by his door. He ended the call and smiled at Nisha.

Queenie, as she walked by the passenger door, pulled her gun as she opened the door and hopped into the vehicle.

The Chinese businessman's eyes opened wider than they probably ever had in his entire life.

Queenie pushed the 357 magnum hard in his side.

Anger replaced his initial shock.

Outwitted and set up by two bitches. What the fuck was wrong with him?

If he could just get to the licensed firearm in his waist…

Nisha opened his door and disarmed him, discreetly slipping it inside her jacket pocket.

"Let's go," she said to Queenie as she slammed the door shut and hurried to her car. Birdman would be pissed. He had instructed them not to take longer than three minutes.

"Drive Chiney bwoy," Queenie told him.

He bristled at the insult.

"Dutty gal…you think you and that bitch going to get away with this? Huh? You know who the fuck I am? Eh gal?"

Queenie smacked him in the face hard with the heavy revolver.

She then placed the gun between his legs.

And pressed down hard.

The Chinese businessman urinated in fear.

"Mi seh drive pussyhole Chiney bwoy," Queenie growled.

She didn't have to repeat herself.

He drove off.

Birdman and Bambino exited the plaza from across the street and pulled off behind them.

Chapter 9

"**M**mmm...fuck me Clive...mmmm....I know you missed this pussy...fuck it...harder!"

Clive groaned as he did as Gina commanded.

He held her by her wide hips and rammed his dick inside her at a ferocious pace.

Her anus got punched repeatedly by his scrotum as he fucked her like a man possessed.

She was right.

He had forgotten how good this pussy felt. Once he had gotten serious with Christine, he had stopped seeing Gina. They had been an item in their final year in college but had broken it off when Clive went to Scotland to do his Masters in civil engineering.

But they never stopped fucking. For those two years they fucked like rabbits whenever he came home for the summer holidays. And it had continued throughout the years, regardless of the fact that were both in relationships. Gina had been pissed when he had told her two years ago that he was now serious about his relationship and was going to be monogamous.

Or at least try to.

He had been doing a good job of being faithful to Christine – even had thoughts of marriage creeping into his head over the past year though he had yet to broach the topic with Christine – and had stayed away so Gina had been very surprised, though pleasantly so, when he had sent her an email saying that he missed her and wanted to see her. Though she had not spoken to him for some time, once he contacted her all the feelings, especially the sexual ones, that she had thought were long gone, came rushing back with a vengeance.

"Yes Clive...you know this is your pussy...that can't change...mmmm...no matter what...ahhh...right there... hitting my spot...coming...coming...ohhhh!"

Gina's voluptuous body shook mightily as she climaxed, bathing Clive's still plunging member with her hot sticky juices.

He groaned. Loudly. He wasn't far behind.

He gritted his teeth and he swore his toes curled as his orgasm rushed to the fore. It was a powerful one. One filled with the frustration of not having sex for over a month. One filled with anger at the way Christine was treating him. One filled with the joy of being inside his sexy ex-girlfriend once again. One filled with the pleasure of knowing that she had missed him so much. He uttered a guttural roar as he spilled a copious amount of semen inside his Durex fuego condom. He loved that brand. Made him feel like he wasn't wearing anything.

"Oh God...fuck Gina...my knees feel weak..."

Gina laughed as she caught her breath. That had good. So *good*. Clive had always been the best lover she had ever had. He could have this pussy anytime he wanted it. *Anytime.* She was certain that even when they were old and grey, and married to their respective spouses, they would still be getting it on.

She turned her head and looked at Clive. She was still in the same position on her knees.

"So...is this a one time trip down memory lane or will I be seeing you from time to time?"

Clive looked at her smooth, dark oval face. Gina was a very pretty, sexy dark-skinned girl. But she was also head-strong and obstinate. And that had been the catalyst for their break-up. The sex had always been phenomenal though. And that had not changed.

"You'll definitely be seeing me every now and then," Clive declared, as he treated her prominent ass to a resounding slap.

"Owww...mmm...don't start anything you can't finish," Gina warned.

Clive chuckled as he extracted his almost flaccid dick from inside her and removed the condom. Gina got turned on immensely by her ass being slapped, hard.

Clive went to use the bathroom and after chatting with Gina for awhile longer, left her apartment. He was participating in a pool tournament in another hour and a half.

Queenie kept her gun pointed at the Chinese business-man's genitals as he drove where she instructed him to go. His face was grim and sweaty as he pondered how he could get out of this situation. He could not allow this bitch to take him somewhere and kill him. He had too much to live for to go out like this.

"If yuh even blink too hard mi ah go shoot off yuh little shrivel up cocky," Queenie told him as though she was reading his mind.

The man didn't answer but he was sweating even more now despite the fact that the air conditioner was on.

"Pull over into that plaza," Queenie instructed.

He did as he was told and placed the vehicle in park.

A few seconds later he was yanked unceremoniously from the vehicle by Danger and one of the other guys and placed inside the car Bambino was driving. He was then tied up and blindfolded.

He panicked.

"I-I-I ca-ca-can give you money...lots of money...just don't kill me! Please! I'm begging you!" he cried.

A hard blow to the head by a miniature aluminum baseball bat quieted him down instantly and immediately gave him a lump on his broad forehead.

"Shut up yuh rass Chiney bwoy," Bambino snarled. "Only speak when spoken to."

Bambino then headed out to a safe house they rented off Molynes Road.

They got there in a few minutes and hauled the silently crying businessman into the house. It was a two bedroom house that Birdman had rented for storage purposes and situations like this where they did not want to go to their home base in the ghetto.

"Oww!" the man cried out as he was thrown on the floor like a sack of potatoes.

"Mi ah go ask a question. Mi ah go only ask it one time. If mi nuh get the correct answer mi ah go use a cutlass and chop off yuh two foot dem and leave yuh in here to bleed to death," Bambino told him as he crouched beside the man.

The Chinese businessman relieved his bladder.

He found it difficult to breathe.

Fear had him in a vice grip.

"However, if yuh answer the question correctly without any problems...then we will let yuh go without hurting yuh," Bambino continued. "Yuh understand?"

The man shook his head vigourously.

"Where can we find de warehouse wid de weed?"

Birdman smiled as he lit his spliff. He was enjoying the proceedings. It was a joy to watch Bambino at work. He loved his job and did it well. And he always got results. Eighteen years old. A fucking criminal prodigy.

The Chinese businessman's body seemed to deflate at Bambino's words. It would really hurt to lose this shipment. Marijuana was scarce right now and he had already received a £25,000 down payment on the order. Fuck! He would have to return the money and endure a substantial loss. He had invested a lot in getting this shipment together. But it wasn't worth his life. He would regroup. And not only that. He would find out who these men were and have them dealt with.

"It's at 56 Harbour Street," he told them as he sighed in resignation.

Downtown Kingston.

"Who is at the warehouse?" Bambino queried.

The man shook his head.

"Nobody is there. The place is locked up tightly so no security is needed."

Bambino looked over at Birdman and smiled.

This was an easy one. Like taking candy from a baby.

"Which part de key deh?" he asked, turning his attention back to the man. His urine was starting to smell in the heat. In another hour or so the sun would be history but at the moment, it was a very hot and humid evening.

"I have it," he responded. "It's on my key ring...my vehicle's key ring."

Bambino rose and told Danger that he and one of the guys should put the Chinese businessman inside the trunk of the car.

"Time fi go pick up our merchandise," Bambino told Birdman.

They then exited the house and Bambino retrieved the key from the man's SUV, locked the vehicle securely and they drove out leaving it in the parking lot. Queenie was now riding with Birdman as they headed downtown. No longer confident that they were going to let him go, and being deathly afraid of close spaces, the Chinese business-man lost control of his bowels by the time the vehicles headed down Molynes Road.

Chapter 10

They arrived at the warehouse on Harbour Street in thirty five minutes. There was a lot of traffic on the road. Trying to navigate Kingston's roads between the hours of 5-7 p.m. meant suffering through bumper to bumper traffic as the majority of Kingston's workforce attempted to get home. The trucker that they had called to meet them there had not yet arrived despite the fact that he had claimed he would have been there in twenty minutes. Bambino hoped for his sake that he got there soon. They did not want to spend any more time at the warehouse than was necessary.

The two vehicles parked directly in front of the warehouse, which from all outward appearances, looked like an abandoned building. Peeling paint, graffiti on the walls, large rusty metallic shutter; one would never imagine the treasure it housed inside.

Bambino handed the key to Danger who opened the locks.

He then lifted the well-oiled shutter with the assistance of one of the other guys.

There was another door to open. A sturdy, blue steel door that looked like it weighed five hundred pounds. The two locks on it opened easily enough and they entered the warehouse.

Bambino checked the wall blindly and found a light switch.

The parcels of weed were on pallets, packaged and ready to go.

They heard a loud noise outside.

The truck had arrived.

"Alright, mek we deal with dis fast," Bambino announced and everyone, including Queenie, started loading the parcels onto the truck.

They worked quickly, and in half an hour, all the marijuana and the added bonus of two barrels - one filled with canned food items and another with baby stuff like pampers and bottles, were also taken. They would give those out in the ghetto for free. Treat the poor and needy to an early Christmas.

They locked back up the warehouse and headed out. They never noticed the security cameras that had recorded their every move.

The Chinese businessman was dumped by the waterfront at Kingston Harbour.

He was still tied and blindfolded.

They headed to Rosewater Meadows in high spirits though Bambino didn't like the fact that Birdman had told him not to kill the Chinese businessman. True, the only persons whose faces he had actually seen were Queenie's and Nisha's, but Bambino still didn't like loose ends.

But all in all, it had been a productive day.

The Chinese businessman was rescued by a passing patrol car five minutes after his captors had left. He had gotten to his feet but didn't move as he didn't know which way to go. His hands were tied behind his back so he was unable to remove the tightly tied black cloth covering his eyes. So he had stood up and shouted for help until he was hoarse.

Fortunately for him, the police saw him when they did, as his shouting had attracted the attention of a homeless man of unsound mind who was not taking kindly to his peace and quiet being disturbed. He had been angrily approaching the shouting man with a piece of steel when the cops showed up.

The police recognized the prominent businessman. Mr. Marcel Chang, owner of several businesses including a chain of furniture stores and reputed drug dealer – if you knew who to ask. He told them that he had been kidnapped by thugs as he left his workplace but that they had let him go after he refused to give them more money than what he had in his vehicle. He did not wish to make an official report. The cops, especially the one that had been in the force for fourteen years, were skeptical but did not press the issue. They gave him a ride to his home despite his filthy, smelly state and graciously accepted the $20,000 and the bottle of champagne that Mr. Chang had offered to them in thanks. The security company that had set up the anti-theft device in his SUV located the vehicle by GPS tracking.

As soon as he got himself cleaned up, he called his gangster friend, an enforcer from the community of Kirk

Lane and told him what had happened. The guy, known as Matrix, was very upset. He promised to meet him at the warehouse downtown. Mr. Chang was too upset to drive so he called one his employees who sometimes doubled as a driver when needed. The fear was now gone. Anger had taken its place. Time for retribution.

They had taken his Rolex, his licensed firearm and his marijuana, and last but not least, his pride. He couldn't wait to go down there and view the tapes. Find out who the fuckers were. They were going to wish they had killed him.

He was positive that the cameras had not been spotted. They were too well hidden. He poured himself a strong drink while he waited for the driver to arrive.

Chapter 11

They went straight to Birdman's lair when they got to Rosewater Meadows. The truck backed into the driveway and they removed the cargo, placing it in a backroom downstairs that Birdman used for storage. The two barrels containing the food and baby items were taken by three of the men down to the community center and dispersed to members of the community who, upon hearing about the free stuff, descended on the community center like a swarm of bees.

"All now mi caa believe how de big man shit up himself," Danger was saying as some of the gang members lounged in Birdman's back yard. They were enjoying the four ounces of marijuana, three bottles of Hennessy and the case of red bull that Birdman had provided. Queenie and Nisha were in the kitchen cooking stew chicken, cornmeal dumplings the size of cartwheels and boiled bananas. Work was over. It was time to unwind and relax.

The men laughed raucously, especially the ones that hadn't been there.

Bambino was chilling but he felt slightly uneasy. He was having that weird feeling. His spirit was troubled. He remembered the first time he had the *feeling*. He was eight years old. Living in a one room shack with his mother in the section of Rosewater Meadows known as 'The Gulf'. It was the most decrepit area in the sprawling ghetto community.

It was 7 p.m. and he had just gotten home from downtown Kingston after a day of hustling in the street. It hadn't been a particularly fruitful day. He had only managed to steal a couple of oranges and $300 which he had grabbed from a vendor giving a customer her change. The overweight vendor could only helplessly shout 'Teef! Teef!' in her loud shrilly tone as he darted through the crowded market. He wasn't very hungry though thankfully, as the owner of a restaurant on East Queen's Street had given him a small box with slightly burnt rice and chicken back as payment for helping to take out the garbage and cleaning the front of the restaurant.

A *feeling* had overcome him as he pushed the zinc gate and entered the tenement yard which housed nine small shacks, and over twenty people. He had cautiously made his way to his home, didn't even try to peek at Miss Cookie, who was at the pipe that the entire yard used as a shower, bathing. A makeshift zinc wall had been erected around the pipe to give a small measure of privacy but it was woefully inadequate.

The door had been slightly open and the light, which they stole from the main line on the road, was on. He had stepped inside the one room shack to find his mother on the mattress on the floor which served as their bed. Her washed out floral dress that she usually wore most days was ripped and bunched around her waist. Her legs were agape. Her panties, which had been black at one time but were now a dull grey, had been pulled to one side, exposing her hairy vagina.

Her eyes were wide open.

She was dead.

Bambino had heard a line the star of a movie he had seen on the small T.V. down by Maas Joe's bar some months ago utter that he had never forgotten.

When you die with your eyes open you deserve it.

His mother hadn't been the best mom on earth but he didn't think that she deserved to die like this. He hadn't cried though. He had been suffering from the moment he exited his mother's womb. Life had been a harsh, uncompromising journey. One that was so rough, bleak and distressing, he didn't have time to be a child. He was only eight but he might as well had been eighteen. He had seen and done things that would cause many grown men sleepless nights.

The room smelled of rum.

Strong, white over-proof rum.

He knew who killed his mother.

Who had choked her to death.

He could see the marks on her brown neck.

He placed the oranges in a box in the corner of the room and headed out to avenge his mother's death. He never liked her men anyway. Especially that drunk bastard whom everyone called Rum Belly. Bambino was certain that he was killer.

He had waited in the dark outside Rum Belly's two room board house that he shared with his common-law-wife and their four kids, one two years older than Bambino, for two hours before being rewarded for his patience when he heard the sound of Rum Belly's drunken, atrocious rendition of a popular hymnal.

Rock of ages
Cleft for me
Let me hide myself in thee

When he got to his gate Bambino grabbed him and stabbed him in the heart, silencing him.

Forever.

The first stab had killed him but Bambino had stabbed him repeatedly, even as he lay dead on the ground, as though he had nine lives and he was extinguishing every one of them.

Now he was experiencing that *feeling* again. Something was wrong. But what it was, he had no idea.

He sipped his drink of Hennessy and took a strong toke of his marijuana joint.

Whatever it was, he would be ready.

"Bumboclaat!" Matrix exclaimed, as he viewed the surveillance tapes at the warehouse with Mr. Chang in the room at the back of the warehouse. The door leading to the room had been cleverly disguised to look like a part of the wall. Matrix had been impressed. He had seen something like that in a movie once.

"Mi know dem! Ah de gang from Rosewater Meadows," he continued. "Watch de one Birdman and pussyhole Bambino."

He hated everyone from the rival community but he had a special dark place in his heart for Bambino. He hated him with a passion. The handsome Indian youth had slept with both his baby mother *and* his sister, despite the fact that the two communities were lethal enemies. It was the stuff of legends.

Matrix had badly embarrassed.

When he found out he had beaten his baby mother so badly that she had to be hospitalized for three weeks. His sister had not escaped his wrath either, and their relationship had never recovered.

This was a fascinating development. God bless technology.

Mr. Chang rubbed his chin as he watched. His eyes narrowed when he saw Queenie. He personally wanted to kill that bitch. She had humiliated him badly.

"So these men are your enemies."

More of a statement than a question. Mr. Chang knew that there was no love lost between the two adjacent communities.

"True yuh nuh know how bad mi wah fi kill dem bwoy deh," Matrix snarled as he watched them remove the parcels of marijuana from the warehouse. "Mi nuh t'ink seh my boss ah go want fi get involve inna dis still enuh Mr. Chang. Is a personal t'ing dis and due to the peace treaty dat the two community sign..."

Mr. Chang waved him off. "That's ok...you've been a big enough help. I know the best way to deal with this."

He took out his mobile and scrolled for the number of a police officer that he knew well.

"Detective Patterson. I trust all is well. I have a big bust for you, in Rosewater Meadows. Come by my house later and we'll discuss the details."

Marcel Chang smiled as he hung up the phone. Detective Patterson was a team player. He would give him the bust but stipulate that half of the marijuana be returned to him as well as that girl in the gang. He wanted to deal with her personally. They could kill everyone else on the spot. Make it look like a shoot out. They did it all the time anyway. He gave Matrix $15,000 for his assistance and they left the warehouse in separate vehicles.

The detective would be meeting with him at his home in another hour.

Chapter 12

"**W**ho dis?" Birdman asked through a mouthful of dumpling and chicken. He didn't recognize the number but had answered anyway.

"Peanuts," the voice replied. "Need fi talk to yuh."

"So talk," Birdman said caustically. What the fuck did Peanuts want?

"Mi *know* seh ah you kill Rhino," Peanuts told him, getting straight to the point. "Yuh double cross de man an' tek him money and yuh also tek something dat belong to mi. Mi want back mi coke."

Birdman stopped chewing. He was shocked. How the hell had Peanuts found out? And what coke was he talking about?

He jumped up from his chair and placed his unfinished meal on the table.

"Weh de fuck yuh ah talk 'bout Peanuts? Which coke? Mi nuh know nothing 'bout no coke." He didn't even try to deny that he had gotten Rhino killed and robbed. What was the use? Peanuts was already convinced and he would have lost face trying to lie. Better to acknowledge it like a true gangster. Let Peanuts know that *he* wasn't afraid of him. But he was perturbed about the cocaine part of it. He remembered his initial surprise when Bambino had told him that all he had found was the money. He glanced over at Bambino. He was eating. He felt Birdman's gaze and their eyes met.

Birdman looked away and walked over to the fence overlooking the gully, away from everyone.

"Don't bloodclaat play dumb Birdman. Mi want mi coke!" Peanuts told him angrily.

"Watch yuh pussyclaat mouth Peanuts! Yuh check seh ah one ah yuh flunky dem yuh ah deal wid? Mi seh mi nuh know nutten 'bout nuh coke. Mi ah go check it out and get back to yuh."

"Get back to mi by tonight. An' one more t'ing… somebody from yuh crew haffi dead as payback fi Rhino."

Birdman was about to retort angrily when he realized that Peanuts had already hung up. He looked over the gully at Kirk Lane. Did Bambino really find cocaine over Rhino's house and keep it for himself? Or was Peanuts lying? Trying to get something out of this seeing as he can't ask for the money as that part of it wasn't his business. They were all crooks. People got double crossed all the time. Big deal. And as for somebody from his crew dying because they had killed Rhino, if it was true that Bambino had lied to him about the cocaine, he would gladly offer him to Peanuts as sacrifice. He sighed as he turned and walked back over to the gathering.

Bambino finished his food and belched loudly. He rose from where he was sitting and went inside the house. He wanted to use the bathroom. He still had the *feeling*. He wondered who had called Birdman. While on the phone he had looked at him with a strange expression. Well, he would know soon enough. Birdman told him most things and if the call had been about him, they would definitely be talking about it sooner than later. He finished peeing and shook his sleeping monster dry. He then turned to wash his hands. Nisha was standing by the open bathroom door.

Her mouth was wide open.

Her eyes were misty with awe, lust and curiosity.

Bambino was impassive as he washed his hands. He chided himself for being so deep in thought that she could have stood there the entire time watching him without him knowing.

Nisha.

Queenie's bad ass half-sister.

Different mothers.

Nineteen years old.

London born and bred. Came to visit her half-sister last year after meeting each other on Myspace. After her first visit she loved her sister's gangster lifestyle so much she came back for the summer and was still in Jamaica with no immediate plans of leaving. She had been thrilled to participate in the kidnapping of the Chinese businessman earlier today. He hadn't really paid her much attention as he knew that Birdman was fucking her. And Birdman was very territorial when it came to women. Even his woman's sister. Bambino could never understand that kind of mentality. So he had ignored her knowing stares and never said more than hi to her.

Bambino dried his hands and moved towards the door.

She didn't move out of his way.

Her eyes said what her trembling mouth couldn't.

What the hell. Fuck it. He was going to sample her ripe, thick nineteen year old frame right here in Birdman's bathroom.

Probably a nice quickie would take the edge off.

He pulled her inside and closed the door.

"Detective Patterson, good to see you man," Mr. Chang greeted as Patterson, accompanied by two of his close friends from the Special Crimes Unit, entered the expansive living room.

They shook hands and he gestured for the men to have a seat. His diminutive wife appeared with a trolley of hard liquor and ice, and disappeared just as quickly.

The men poured the drink of their choice and Mr. Chang got down to business. He told them about his kidnapping, omitting certain details such as defecating on himself, and the subsequent robbery. He then advised them that he would give them the bust, but would require that he retain half of the marijuana and that the men be killed. There had been two women involved but he wanted one in particular – if possible.

Detective Patterson nodded agreeably. He knew Birdman and his gang well. Knew the girl too. Birdman's main girl and partner in crime. He had received money from Birdman on more than one occasion. Had even sold a motorcycle to the ruthless young buck Bambino.

But he didn't have a problem killing them. Business was business. Besides, they were responsible for several murders across the corporate area and numerous other crimes. He would be doing society a favour by punching their tickets tonight. And the bust would look good on the evening news tomorrow.

"How much?" he asked Chang as he drained his glass. He loved Johnny Walker Black Label. A man's drink.

"One hundred thousand," Chang replied.

"One fifty," Patterson countered.

"Alright…but only if you bring the girl here alive."

"Fair enough. We'll strike later tonight."

They shook hands and the meeting was over.

Chapter 13

"Ohhhh! Fuck! Bloody hell!" Nisha shouted as Bambino fucked her doggystyle. She was in front of the sink balancing with one hand on the wall and her left leg planted on the toilet seat.

She was looking at herself in the mirror.

She didn't recognize the face staring back at her. The veins in her forehead were pronounced and her mouth was twisted in a frightening sneer. Her eyes bulged with each powerful stroke. Her breathing was shallow and ragged. And the grunts she was emitting with each thrust would put a pig to shame.

She half expected to see his dick exit through her mouth.

Her pussy was on fire.

It burned.

It hurt.

It throbbed.

It pulsed.

It ached.

It felt like it didn't belong to her.

She was so wet.

Wetter than she had ever been in her life.

She came.

Again.

Third time in ten minutes.

One more and her face would smash into the mirror from fainting.

"Break me in two you fucking wanker! Oh God! Fuck me! Tear up this cunt! Bloody fucking hell! Oh sweet Jesus!"

This was really going to be a quick one.

Her pussy was good – tight and fleshy – though at his size almost any pussy would feel tight.

Her dirty talk in that sexy British accent was threatening to push him over the edge.

It stopped threatening and pushed.

He grunted as he spilled his seed inside her.

"Yes! Yes! Yessss!" Nisha screamed as she climaxed hard. Feeling his thick hot juices being sprayed inside her had intensified her orgasm.

She felt dizzy.

But before she could finish savouring the moment, the bathroom door flew open.

It was Birdman.

"But ah weh de bumboclaat dis ah gwaan inna mi house?" he queried angrily, glaring at the sweaty, partially clothed, satiated twosome.

Clive arrived at the pool hall a few minutes late. The tournament had already begun but fortunately he got there in time before it was his turn to play. He went over by his friends to say hi. He didn't see Robbie, his best friend and partner in crime. He reached in his pocket for his cell phone. It wasn't there. He tried to remember the last time he had used it. About two hours ago when his little brother had called him begging money. Shit. He must have inadvertently left it at Gina's. He borrowed one of his friends' mobile and dialed his number.

Gina answered on the third ring.

"Hey Gina, it's me," he said.

"Hi Clive," Gina responded chirpily. "You left your phone on the sofa…guess it had fallen out of your pocket in your rush to tear my clothes off."

They both chuckled.

"Bring it to the sports bar on Hagley Park road…I'm playing in a tournament for the next few hours."

"Ok no problem, I was just getting ready to meet up with one of my girlfriends in New Kingston for drinks. I'll drop it off on my way."

"Ok, thanks sexy. Later."

Gina smiled as she hung up the phone. This reunion was different. She was feeling butterflies like she used to back in the day when they were so in love. She liked the feeling. She wondered what it would be like to get back together with Clive again. Maybe some of the problems they used to have back in the day they wouldn't have now as they had both grown in so many ways. It was worth a shot. Just one problem. Clive was in a relationship. She was in one too but she could drop Roderick at any time. He was ok but she wouldn't lose a night's sleep over leaving him.

She checked her face in the mirror one last time, and pleased with what she saw; she grabbed her pocketbook and headed out. Clive's phone rang just as she was about to drive out. She looked at it. A picture of an attractive light-skinned girl was on the screen. She was stored as *Babes*. Must be his girlfriend.

Gina smiled devilishly and pressed the answer button.

Nisha's eyes widened in fright. She knew she was loud when she was enjoying sex but she hadn't expected anyone to barge into the bathroom.

She looked at Birdman defiantly. He was furious but she didn't give a fuck. He wanted to have his cake and eat it. He had to hide the fact that he was sleeping with her yet he didn't want her seeing anyone. He was sleeping with her against her will but if she wanted to hang around the gang, and she very much did, she had no choice but to give in to him whenever he managed to corner her.

"Bambino! Wah de bloodclaat dis? Eeh? Wah kind ah disrespect dis?" Birdman demanded.

Bambino was unimpressed. He knew the real reason Birdman was tripping. He had slept with numerous women before at Birdman's house but his jealousy over Nisha was making him act like a punk.

Bambino slowly removed his lengthy, now almost flaccid tool from inside of Nisha and pulled up his boxers and jeans. His face was stoic as he looked at Birdman.

"Weh yuh mean what a gwaan? Yuh blind? Mi and Nisha just done fuck. Weh yuh ah gwaan so fah?"

Birdman lost it.

He stepped up closer to Bambino shouting that he would rather die than let anybody disrespect him in his own fucking house.

Queenie as well as some of the other gang members heard the ruckus and came to investigate.

"Birdman! Bambino! What the fuck is going on?" Queenie asked. She looked in the bathroom and saw that Nisha was in there. She was still fixing her clothes.

Queenie sighed. How Nisha could take Bambino's dick was beyond her. She had seen it one day and almost fainted. But why was Birdman so angry?

"De bwoy Bambino ah dis de program! Inna mi blood-claat bathroom ah fuck yuh sister!"

Queenie was confused. Bambino had done stuff like that at the house many times before. So what was the problem now?

"So what? That is nothing new so why yuh acting like that?"

Birdman turned around in anger at Queenie's words and administered a vicious slap to her face.

"Shut up yuh bloodclaat mouth!" he thundered. He just couldn't get the sound of Nisha's passionate cries out of his head. She had never made those sounds when *he* was having sex with her. Always quiet and acted as though she couldn't wait for him to get off of her. The sight of Bambino's massive unsheathed tool, slick with Nisha's juices, pulling out of her tight pussy that he loved so much, had placed him in an uncontrollable rage.

He slapped Queenie again.

She cried out in pain.

"Wah dat fah! Yuh ah behave like yuh jealous ah mi bloodclaat sister. So what if yuh friend have sex with her. She's a big fucking woman. What the fuck do you care?"

Birdman jumped on her and rained powerful blows on her face and torso.

The men held him and pulled him off of her.

"Easy boss...easy man..." Danger said as he helped two of the men hold back Birdman.

Bambino had seen enough.

He roughly moved through the crowd and left the house.

"Hey bumbohole! Weh yuh t'ink yuh ah go?" Birdman shouted at Bambino's retreating back.

Bambino did not stop or look back.

Queenie got up from off the floor holding her jaw.

An alarm went off in her head.

There could only be one reason for Birdman's jealous rage.

He was fucking her sister!

Her tear stained, slightly swollen face registered disbelief.

"Nisha? Jesus Christ! Yuh really fuck mi man? Eeh Nisha?"

Nisha's face clouded with shame.

"Hey gal stop chat fuckery!" Birdman shouted as he tried to break free from his men to attack her again.

Queenie didn't look at him. She only had eyes for Nisha who was looking at her and shaking her head with tear-filled eyes. "I-I-I didn't want to Queenie! I swear t-t-o God...he forced me innit?"

Queenie turned away with a wounded cry and rushed upstairs to get her gun. She was going to kill somebody tonight.

Chapter 14

"**H**ello?"

The voice sounded surprised and annoyed.

Christine moved the phone from her ear and checked the number again. Yep, it was Clive's number.

"Yes? Hello," Gina responded airily. She was enjoying this.

"Let me speak to Clive."

"Clive doesn't have his phone right now but you can call him back in about half an hour. He left it accidentally."

"Is that right...and who are you?" Christine queried frostily.

"It escapes me how that's any of your business. Like I said, call him back in about half an hour."

Gina then hung up and headed out.

She was smiling.

She had thoroughly enjoyed that little exchange.

Christine was livid when she realized that the person had hung up on her. *Calm down Chrissy,* she mused. *Calm down.* She took a deep breath as she paced the living room. She absolutely hated people being rude to her and that bitch, whoever she was, had been very rude. She told herself that the person must be either one of Clive's co-workers or friends. If it was anything else Clive could not have been so uncaring or stupid to be throwing it in her face. She had thought about their argument and had decided to be the bigger person and try to move on from it. So she had decided to call and invite him over for a nightcap. They could talk about things and who knows; maybe she would have even given him some. That was out the window now. That feisty bitch had ruined it. Like they say, no good deed goes unpunished.

Bambino walked out to the road and saw a taxi parked by a woman's gate. The taxi driver was standing by the woman's gate talking to her. Whatever he was saying seemed to be very amusing. The woman was in stitches, her large stomach rolling with each raucous laugh. Bambino walked over to him. His house was only a fifteen minute walk away over the other side of Rosewater Meadows but he didn't feel like walking and he was not driving any of Birdman's vehicles home. He couldn't believe the way Birdman had behaved. The little respect he had for him had gone right out the window. The only way he would have anything to do with Birdman anymore was if he apologized profusely for his behaviour.

He could still hear the shouting in the house.

He looked at the taxi driver. He didn't recognize him though he could never be a stranger and be here at this time.

Strange men did not venture into Rosewater Meadows after dark.

"Yo! Drop me over on Lewis Drive," Bambino said brusquely and opened the back door.

"But ah wah dis? Ah so yuh talk to big man youth? Lock mi car door man! Yuh nuh 'ave nuh manners," the taxi driver responded, not noticing the signals the woman was frantically giving him. "Bright and out of order."

The taxi driver had only been living in Rosewater Meadows for two weeks. His brother, who had lived there for over twenty years, was ill and had asked him to run his cab for him until he got back on his feet.

Bambino did as the man told him and shut the door. He then walked around the car and approached the man.

"Bambino...him nuh really know betta....jus' cool...mi ah beg fi him," the woman pleaded.

Bambino ignored her and whipped out his desert eagle.

The man's eyes widened. He opened his mouth to say something and Bambino slid the gun inside his mouth.

"Nuh kill 'im Bambino...please...mi ah beg fi him Bambino...'im just neva know seh ah yuh run t'ings," the woman begged tearfully.

She had just met the man two days ago and had really taken a liking to him. She was even planning to give him some tomorrow night.

Bambino looked at the fear in the man's eyes.

It was a look that he had seen countless times.

Though he was not in the best of moods and even though ignorance was no excuse, he decided to chill.

He removed the gun from the man's mouth.

Slowly.

Then he opened the back door and got in.

The man, after breathing a heavy sigh of relief, quickly hopped in and took Bambino to his destination.

Just as Queenie retrieved her 9 mm handgun from her bedside drawer and turned around, Birdman was right there to take it from her. They struggled mightily and Birdman had to really fight her like he would a man in order to disarm her. After several hard punches to the gut, Queenie finally released the gun and fell to the ground in pain holding her stomach.

Breathing heavily, Birdman stood over her menacingly. She would have to be severely punished. Talking to him so disrespectfully in front of his crew. Acting up and making a bad situation worse. She needed to be reminded who was in charge. But he would deal with her later. He removed the other two guns that were in the room, and left, locking the bedroom door and pocketing the key. He would return in a few hours and teach her a lesson that she wouldn't forget anytime soon. There was someone else who needed to be reminded who was boss. And also answer a few questions. And he better get the right answers.

"Someone called for you just as I was entering the car... I answered by accident. She sounded pissed. Sorry about that," Gina said sweetly as she handed the phone to Clive. They were standing outside of the pool hall. Clive had just won his first game when he looked up and saw some of the guys leering at a tall, dark voluptuous beauty. Gina had arrived. He had hugged her and led her outside.

Clive took the phone and looked at his received calls. Christine.

He smiled at Gina. "It's ok."

"Ok, sweets, good. I wouldn't want to cause any problems."

She kissed him on the lips. "I gotta run...see you soon."

He slapped her ass as she walked away.

She stuck her tongue out at him and disappeared down the stairs.

Clive smiled and returned Christine's call. He guessed she had realized the error of her ways and had called to apologize. He looked over the balcony at Gina as she walked towards her car. Damn she was sexy. He knew she had deliberately answered his phone. He didn't mind though. Maybe a little jealously was just what Christine needed to make her start acting like a woman again. *His* woman.

"Hello sir," Christine said when she answered the phone. She was online checking her Facebook account. She commented on one of her old school mates' pictures.

"What's up...you had called for me earlier."

"Yeah I had called." She added the 'hug me' application to her page.

"So what's up?" Clive reiterated.

"Nothing much…just online," she replied nonchalantly. She was waiting for him to explain who the person was that had answered his phone.

Clive sighed. She was upset. Probably wanted to know who had answered his phone. Well, no information would be forthcoming. He was his own big man. And in light of her recent behaviour, she didn't deserve his nice side right now.

"Ok well, you seem to be ok so I'm going to get back to my pool tournament."

Fuck you! Aloud she said, "Knock yourself out. Bye."

Clive shook his head as he placed the phone in his pocket and went back inside the pool hall. Christine was going to continue until this little spat got out of hand. She really needed to get her act together.

Christine signed out of Facebook and went into the bathroom to take a shower. She just couldn't understand why Clive was acting like Mr. Tough Guy all of a sudden. The word sorry was no longer in his vocabulary. Explanations were no longer a thing of necessity. Not allowing arguments to fester was no longer important. She stripped down and looked at herself critically in the full length mirror. She had let herself go a little since her sister's death but she still looked hot and sexy. Lost a little weight but it wasn't unattractive. She was still kind of thick in the right places. She touched her vagina. She needed to shave.

She also needed to change her hair style. Maybe get a nice short, trendy cut. She would go and see Amelia, her hairdresser, tomorrow.

Get her hair and nails done.

Start back the gym.

Get back to normal.

Ignore Clive and his bullshit.

Follow the doctor's advice.

Stress is the enemy he had said.

He was so right.

And right now Clive represented stress.

A break was in order.

Chapter 15

"**B**ambino! Yo Bambino!"
He had just taken a quick shower and was in the bedroom getting dressed when he heard the shouting in his yard. He recognized the voice. It was Danger. He was sure that there were several of them out there. Birdman would never send just one or two men to come and get him. He was pissed that Bambino had just walked away. He had sent these guys to bring him back. Bambino laughed to himself. Picture that with a fucking Kodak.

"Bambino! Bambino!"

Then his mobile started to ring.

Birdman.

Apparently they had told him that he was inside the house and was ignoring them.

Bambino answered the call.

"Yo ah idiat t'ing yuh keep up today. And we haffi address dat. But even more serious. Mi get a call from Peanuts. Him find out seh ah we kill an' rob Rhino an' seh mi tek him coke. Dat mean *you* tek him coke. And dat mean yuh lie to mi! Because mi ask you point blank if yuh find anyt'ing else inna de house and yuh seh no. We haffi address dat as well. De man dem outside ah wait fi escort yuh back to de house. Mek *sure* yuh bring de coke."

He then hung up.

Bambino continued to get dressed. So this was what the *feeling* had been about. An impending showdown with Birdman. He looked at himself in the mirror. He looked good. Like he was about to go to a party. He was wearing black patent leather hi top Nikes, a pair of black fitted Antik jeans and a black Christian Audigier T-shirt with a flaming skull design. He briefly admired the Rolex watch that he had taken from the Chinese businessman. It looked good on his wrist.

He pulled a large duffle bag and another smaller bag from underneath the bed and transferred all of the cash from the small bag into the large duffle bag. He had eleven thousand dollars in US currency and three hundred and fifty thousand Jamaican dollars in total. He then stuffed two outfits inside his Louis Vuitton backpack along with a few toiletries. He then made sure his two handguns, a desert eagle and a glock 45, were fully loaded.

He looked around the room. He wasn't the sentimental type but he wondered if he would ever see this room again after tonight. When he stepped through the door, anything could happen. In the blink of an eye everything had changed. Birdman had found out about the cocaine. Then there was the drama with Nisha. There was just no coming back from all of this. He placed the backpack on his back and took up the duffle bag. He then turned off the lights and exited the house.

Bambino locked his front door and turned around.

Six members of the gang, including Danger, were in his small yard.

Danger had a smirk on his ugly, pockmarked face. Danger had a face that only a mother could love. Bambino always teased him that the only thing dangerous about him was his ugly face.

Bambino knew that Danger was reveling in the moment. He always hated the way Bambino was allowed to order everyone around and basically do what he wanted. He hated the way Bambino's name was revered in the ghetto. Even his enemies respected him.

"Yuh have de coke?" Danger asked. He had to make sure. Birdman had warned him that he would hold him personally responsible if Bambino came without it.

Bambino nodded to the bag in his hand.

Danger gestured to one of the men to retrieve the bag from Bambino.

The look Bambino gave him stopped him in his tracks.

"Pussyhole don't pass yuh place. Birdman tell oonu seh fi come escort mi to de house, nothing more, nothing less," Bambino declared.

He then walked over to his motorcycle and strapped the duffle bag to the back of the seat.

"Yo weh yuh ah do? Go inna de van," Danger said.

"Go suck yuh madda Danger," Bambino said and hopped onto the bike. He put on his helmet and started the engine.

If looks could kill Bambino would have been a dead man. But it couldn't so Danger merely scowled and told him to ensure that he rode between the two vehicles all the way to Birdman's house. They blocked his exit from the yard until they got into their vehicles. The lead vehicle then headed out and Bambino followed, flanked by the Mitsubishi Sportero driven by Danger.

Bambino waited until they were passing by the main entrance and exit to Rosewater Meadows to make his move. A car was coming from the opposite direction. Timing it perfectly, Bambino swerved dangerously in front of it and turned onto the road that led out of Rosewater Meadows. The extra seconds were all he needed. The well-tuned engine sang a powerful soprano as Bambino pushed the motorcycle to the limit and sped away from his would be captors. He even popped a wheelie for good measure as Danger, though trying desperately to follow, watched helplessly as Bambino disappeared out of sight.

Chapter 16

"**W**ah de fuck yuh mean 'im get weh?" Birdman was incredulous. He was sitting outside in the backyard drinking with two members of the gang eagerly awaiting Bambino's arrival, when the crew had returned empty handed with an I'm-so-fucking-stupid look on their faces. He was dying to make an example of Bambino to the gang. Show them what happened to people brave enough to double cross him. His pride was also wounded. There was a gaping hole where his ego used to be. Bambino's decision to take the cocaine and keep it for himself showed beyond a measure of doubt that he didn't fear him. Or even respect him. Bambino having sex with Nisha, whom he knew that he was sleeping with and liked very much, in his home no less, had really left a bitter taste in his mouth. He wanted revenge. And he wanted it now. Yet Danger, with his crocodile face, was standing before him saying the inconceivable.

The six men standing before him fidgeted but no one responded. They were really ashamed that Bambino had outsmarted them and got away.

"Six bumboclaat so called gangster go fi *one* man and couldn't bring him back. Eeh? Danger! Yuh was in charge. Explain wah de fuck happen."

Danger looked at Birdman's right hand nervously. It was holding an Uzi. One spray from the deadly sub-machine gun and all six of them would be cut down instantly like blades of grass. He didn't want to die. With Bambino now out of favour with the gang and marked for death, he would be second in command. And if by a stroke of luck something was to happen to Birdman, *he* would be the don.

He just had to find a way to survive this.

He took a deep breath and told Birdman how the escape had unfolded. He then quickly followed that up with a passionate plea that he be given a chance to find Bambino and bring him back in a body bag.

Birdman stared at him for what seemed like an eternity.

He was extremely upset and more than a bit perturbed at the thought of Bambino on the loose. His life was in danger. All their lives were. Knowing Bambino, he would be back one day to try and take control of Rosewater Meadows. Bambino was a formidable enemy to have. He had to be found, and quickly. In the meantime, he needed as many bodies as possible to keep around for added protection. That was the only reason he didn't kill all six of them right now.

"Alright Danger...yuh ass deh pon de line trust mi. Yuh betta find him fast. Inna de meantime put the word out dat Bambino rob the gang and run off pon 'im own. He's to be killed pon sight and anybody from Rosewater dat is even rumored to be in touch wid 'im...ah go dead instantly."

Danger, breathing a sigh of relief, got on his mobile and delegated the responsibility of getting the word out to a junior member of the gang who was stationed at the community center where the gang sold their drugs.

Birdman shook his head grimly. He should have killed Bambino when he had the chance.

Randy's iPhone buzzed loudly like a swarm of angry bees from its perch on the dining table. He indicated for one the young ladies present to go and get it for him. She brought the phone back, handed it to him and resumed her position on the cushion in front of him. She took his scrotum in her mouth and stroked him with her right hand as he answered the call.

"Hello," Randy said with his eyes closed. This new girl certainly gave good head. He had met her last night at a private party in Beverly Hills. White college girl from Baltimore who transported drugs for one of his peers from time to time. He had bragged about her oral prowess so Randy had taken her home to find out for himself.

Jenna and Halle, the two young fifteen year old bi-sexual best friends from the affluent suburb of Norbrook who loved to hang out at his place, were playing with each other as they watched the woman pleasure him with her wide mouth.

"Yo Randy. Ah Bambino. Need yuh help."

Bambino was sitting on his bike at the side of the road in Half-Way-Tree. He had pulled over to give Randy a call. A huge electronic advertising billboard up high in front of him was showing the latest cars from the Mercedes Benz dealership.

Randy opened his eyes but did not stop the girl. She was watching him with vivid green eyes as she sucked him languidly. Her lips were thick and juicy like Angelina Jolie's. That was where the resemblance ended, however.

"What's up Bambino?" Randy replied. Bambino was calling in that favour quicker than expected. But it was cool though. He was already making some serious returns on the cocaine that Bambino had sold him at such a low wholesale price. Besides he liked Bambino. He was cool. All about his business. He would help him. If he could.

"Mi need somewhere fi stay uptown fi awhile…starting now," Bambino told him.

Randy thought for a moment. He owned an apartment in Havendale that the tenant, an employee for a US firm that had business interests in Jamaica, had vacated three days ago. His three month tenure in Jamaica had ended and he had returned to the States. It was an apartment that Randy usually rented to non-residents and the rent was quoted in US dollars. It was never empty for long and he was already evaluating several people who had quickly responded to the ad he had placed in the classifieds.

Bambino was lucky. It would cost him though.

"You're a lucky man Bambino…one of my tenants just

vacated an apartment in Havendale three days ago. You can stay there. USD$750 a month, utilities included."

"Nuh problem," Bambino replied. He would probably only be there for a month. He'd lay low for the entire month of December. Just chill, relax and have some fun at some of those uptown spots that he had never been to. Then, as the New Year rolled around, he would handpick a few street soldiers that he knew and head back to Rosewater Meadows and take control of the community. With the right guys backing him up, all he needed was some serious firepower and that wouldn't be a problem to get. "Mi ah come over now fi de key."

"Alright...see you in a bit," Randy replied, breathing heavily. His scrotum was tingling. Damn she was good. She hadn't even been blowing him for five minutes.

The call ended just in time.

His toes curled and he emitted a primal roar as he climaxed with much fanfare. She moaned loudly as she swallowed every drop.

The joint military and police team, led by Detective Patterson and two other members of the Special Crimes Unit, entered Rosewater Meadows in four tinted un-marked vehicles. The twelve cops were in the three Toyota Corollas and the six soldiers were in the Mitsubishi Pajero. Only Patterson and the two cops that had accompanied him to Marcel Chang's home knew about the deal. As far as the others were concerned, this was a drug bust where they would be facing dangerous armed criminals. Orders were to kill if necessary. Patterson was going to ensure that it would be necessary.

They arrived at Birdman's property and one vehicle, the Mitsubishi Pajero, blocked the road a few meters away from Birdman's gate, just in case reinforcements from the gang tried to surprise them when the shooting started. Two of the soldiers, armed with submachine guns, stood guard there. Everyone else rushed onto the property.

"Police! Don't move!" they shouted as they went around to the back of the house.

Birdman, who was on the phone, pacing with the Uzi still in his hand, received the first bullet which shattered his fingers.

"Bumboclaat!" Birdman shouted in shock as a barrage of bullets made him do a drunken dance. He had recognized Patterson. He fell to the ground on his confused face, dead before his body hit the moist grass.

The rest of the gang on the premises sprang into action. They returned fire as they tried to escape. Danger, though firing wildly as he ran towards the gully, managed to hit one the cops in the neck, just above his bulletproof vest, before he was cut down by a precise shot to the back of the head by one of the soldiers as he attempted to jump the fence.

Patterson entered the house via the kitchen. He had already killed two people. He didn't see anyone so he stealthily made his way upstairs. He checked the first bedroom. It was empty. The second door was locked.

"Police! Open up!" he shouted.

Not getting a response, he shot the lock off and entered the room with a shooting stance. He was just in time to see Queenie going through the window.

"Stop bitch!" he shouted. Right now she was worth fifty thousand dollars and he didn't want to have to kill her. He rushed over and pulled her back in. He succeeded and they tumbled onto the floor.

"You?" Queenie cried in surprise as she stabbed Patterson in the neck with the knife she had in her hand. His eyes bulged in shock and pain.

No! This can't be happening! He mused in a daze as his body felt numb with pain. She twisted the knife in the wound before pulling it out. He screamed in agony and managed to squeeze off two shots as she stabbed him in the left eye. Queenie fell on top of him. She was dead. He could still hear shots being fired outside. The gangsters were fighting for dear life.

His last conscious thought was that he wouldn't be able to collect his one hundred and fifty thousand.

Damn.

Chapter 17

Bambino rode into the gated apartment complex on Morningside Drive in Havendale. He had used the gate opener to get in, ignoring the curious stare of the security guard. He parked his motorcycle in front of Apartment 5. He looked around. It was a nice complex. Sixteen one and two bedroom apartments. There was a community pool and a small playground. And best of all, it was gated. Strangers couldn't come and go as they pleased. Suited him just fine.

Like a true businessman, Randy had taken his payment for this month's rent up front when he handed over the keys and gate opener. He had noted that Randy had three women there this time; the two he had seen on his previous visit and a new white one with an intriguingly wide mouth. He wondered absently if Randy would mind sending her over. He wouldn't mind blowing off some steam.

He unstrapped the duffle bag and slung it over his shoulder.

He felt eyes on him and looked to his right. A young woman was standing by a dark blue Honda Civic at Apartment 6. She was looking at him with a surprised expression. She was attractive. Had a very nice shape. She was wearing black leggings with a short silver dress and black stilettos. There was something familiar about her though he was sure he had never met or seen her before. Another young lady came out of the apartment and they both got into the car. She said something to her companion and they both looked at him as she drove off.

Bambino then opened the door and went in. He was very curious about the way she had stared at him. The last thing he needed was somebody recognizing him right off the bat before he even got settled in. His cell phone rang. He didn't recognize the number. He answered the call.

It was Nisha.

"He's hot for real," Miranda said to Christine as they headed out of the complex. Christine had suggested that they get out of the house so they decided to go to New Kingston to have a few drinks.

"Yeah, he's very handsome. It's the guy I was telling you about that I saw slap the big man in his face the other day when I was having lunch on the strip."

"Mr. Coleman went back to the States the other day… maybe he's our new neighbour," Miranda speculated.

Christine thought about that as they headed down Mannings Hill road. Now that would be a strange twist of fate. She hadn't even expected to see him again much less to have him as a neighbour. She thought about him all the way to New Kingston.

"Bloody hell Bambino! The cops came here and there was a shootout yeah. Queenie is dead! I think everybody is dead!"

"Slow down Nisha...wah yuh really ah seh?"

Nisha told him everything that happened since he left the house. Birdman had beat up Queenie and locked her in their bedroom. He had beaten her up too. Her face was swollen and her right eye was badly bruised. She had stayed in the bathroom crying for a long time then she had heard gunshots outside and lots of shouting. She had turned off the bathroom light and hid in the shower until it had subsided. Then she had cautiously made her way to Queenie's bedroom and saw her dead on the floor with one of the cops lying next to her. He was also dead. Had a knife sticking out of his left eye. She was afraid as the cops were still around, she could hear them talking outside. She didn't want to be discovered.

Bambino was shocked at what he was hearing. What had prompted the cops to make a raid on the camp? Why hadn't any of their contacts in the force called and warned them? He hadn't missed any calls and they had no way of already knowing that he and the gang had fallen out. Birdman was probably dead. His only regret about that was that he had been robbed of the opportunity to do it himself. Life was so funny. The only reason he was probably alive now was because he and the gang had fallen out. He would have been there under normal circumstances. Guess it wasn't his time to go just yet. He was surprised to find himself feeling relieved. Did he actually care whether he lived or died? Not so long ago the answer would have been an emphatic no, now he wasn't so sure anymore. He told Nisha to pack a light bag with some clothes and her travel documents, and lay low until she could leave the house undetected.

He told her the fun was over for now and that she should try and return to England as soon as possible. They spoke for awhile longer then he ended the call and called one of his police contacts. Detective Patterson's phone rang without an answer. He called Deidre. She answered on the first ring.

"Jesus Christ! Bambino? Yuh alive! Mi hear seh yuh did dead too!" she exclaimed.

Bambino asked her to tell him everything she knew about what had happened.

She told him that Rosewater Meadows was under curfew until 9 a.m. tomorrow. The place was teeming with cops and word was that Birdman, his girl, Danger and about ten other gang members had been killed in the shootout. Two cops had been killed as well. Bambino told her to give him a call tomorrow and update him on the situation. She promised to do so and Bambino terminated the call.

He sat down on the couch in the living room and turned on the T.V.

It had been a very eventful day.

Marcel Chang watched the news as he ate his breakfast of whole wheat cereal and orange juice the following morning. The bust and shootout in Rosewater Meadows was the main story. He was disappointed that Patterson had gotten himself killed but he had noted that the marijuana seized was 500 lbs and not 1000. That meant that one of the cops that had accompanied Patterson to meet him was enterprising enough to still carry out the deal or – and he hoped fervently that this was not the case – was going to keep it for himself. He would just have to wait and see. The girl, Queenie, had been killed. Too bad. He didn't hear a certain name among the casualties though. Bambino. Had he escaped? Hopefully, if and when the cop contacted him, he could find out what happened to the one called Bambino. He didn't want any of them that were involved in his kidnapping to be free roaming the streets. He swallowed the last of his orange juice and grabbed his attaché case. He exited the house and got into his SUV. He really hoped the cop got in touch with him soon.

Bambino didn't get out of bed until 1 p.m. He was famished. He took a quick shower and got dressed in one of the two outfits that he had managed to take with him.

He needed to go shopping. All of his gear was at home in Rosewater Meadows. He counted out $60,000 and placed the coil in his pocket. He then headed out. First he would get some food and then do some shopping. He didn't plan to stay cooped up in the house everyday so he needed to get some clothes.

He went to a Chinese restaurant on Constant Spring road and had a very enjoyable meal of sweet and sour chicken and shrimp fried rice. He took the waitress' phone number when she came by for the fourth time to check if he was ok. She was sexy. Filled out her black skirt in a very appealing manner. Face was average but she was far enough away from being ugly. She got off at 5:30. Maybe he would scoop her up later. If he didn't, he would probably never call her. He lost interest easily. It was now or never. That was the way he rolled. He finished his meal and left his payment on the table. He left her a nice tip.

The early afternoon sun was ripe as he hopped onto his motorcycle and headed into traffic. There was a store in Half-Way-Tree where he could get his clothes and another one on the other side of the same mall where he could get some foot wear. That suited him just fine. He hated having to visit multiple stores to get what he wanted.

It was 4 p.m. before Marcel Chang got the call that he had been waiting for.

"Mr. Chang, how yuh doing? This is Corporal Crooks, came by your house with Detective Patterson yesterday."

Chang waved his secretary out of his office animatedly. She hurriedly stepped out and closed the door.

"I was hoping I would get this call," Chang responded. "Meet me by the house this evening at 7. Shame what happened to Patterson eh?"

"Yeah, he was a good man," Corporal Crooks replied solemnly.

Crooks told him that he had gotten his cell number from out of Patterson's phone. Chang told him that he was grateful that he had the tenacity to see the deal through and told him that he looked forward to working with him from time to time.

Chang smiled as he hung up the phone. The appropriately named Corporal Crooks seemed to be an able replacement for Detective Patterson. As they say, all's well that ends well.

Christine had just parked her vehicle and was about to go inside when she heard the roar of a motorbike. It was *him.* And he was not alone. She watched as the girl, dressed in the work attire of Little China, her favourite restaurant to get Chinese cuisine, hopped off the back of the beautiful machine. She had never seen her before though. Maybe she had just started working there. He glanced at her with a stoic expression and then went inside his apartment with the young woman behind him. The girl wasn't pretty but had a very nice body. Was she his girlfriend? A handsome guy like that could do much better. She wondered why she even cared. She fished for her keys and went inside. She really needed to stop staring so much whenever she saw him. It was very unbecoming and quite unlike her. She stripped down and immediately went into the bathroom to take a shower. Today had been a miserable day at work but at least she had managed to leave early and get her hair and nails done. She hadn't bothered to cut it as short as she had originally planned. It was now sitting on her shoulders and had subtle but effective red streaks. It looked hot. Apparently her new neighbour wasn't impressed. He had looked at her as though she was wearing rollers. She was offended.

Bambino didn't waste any time. He led her straight to the bedroom and took her clothes off. The girl, Antoinette, stood beside the bed nervously. She had no idea how she was so taken by the quiet, handsome young man. Something about him had permeated her brain and seeped all the way down, eventually settling between her thick, curvy thighs. And now she was at his place. Naked and ready to fuck without as much as twenty sentences having been exchanged between them.

Bambino looked at her as he quickly removed his clothes. She had a really hot body. Flat enough stomach, small perky breasts with nipples the size of ackee seeds, small waist, thick luscious thighs and a very plump mound that was neatly trimmed. He smiled at her expression when his manhood came into view. She looked like she wanted to bolt through the door, leaving her clothes behind.

"B-b-b-ut I can't manage that," she whimpered. She couldn't believe a dick could be that big.

Bambino pulled her to him in response. He reached down and slipped a finger between her legs and inside her wetness. He fingered her as he sucked her large, erect nipples. He slipped in another finger and she groaned and clutched him. He fingered her until she climaxed. He removed his sticky fingers and placed them on her lips. She looked at him wide-eyed as she hesitantly licked them, tasting herself for the very first time.

She felt like she was in a trance.

Marching to the beat of his hypnotic drum.

He pulled her head to his chest and she claimed his right nipple, sucking and licking it until she elicited a low moan from him.

He quickly rolled a condom on and turned her around, bending her over the bed.

"No...its going to hurt...no...fuck me another way... please...I – "

Bambino entered her slowly, choking her in mid-sentence. Antoinette could literally feel him stretching her past capacity and bruising her sugar walls as he slowly gave her his full length.

"Fuck...oh God...no...no...can't manage...Bambino... it hurt so bad..."

Bambino pushed it in to the hilt and let it marinate inside her pulsating wetness for a few seconds before he began to move. He moved slowly at first, giving her a chance to become familiar with the gigantic foreign object that was embedded in previously unchartered territory somewhere deep inside her. She wondered what she hell she had gotten herself into. She had a new found respect for her pussy. She still couldn't believe that she was taking all of it.

"Bumboclaat!" she shrieked as he picked up the pace a notch, slapping her ample ass with each never-ending stroke. "Fuck! You're going to split me in two Bambino! Oh God! Help me Jesus!"

Bambino was impervious to her screams. He held on to her hips and clicked into high gear, thrusting rapidly.

Her passionate cries, coated with pain, clicked into high gear as well. She sounded like a wounded opera singer.

She hit and sustained a high note of which Mariah Carey would have been proud as Bambino hit a spot that she was certain was somewhere close to her lungs and the resulting orgasm was so sudden and unexpected that she didn't know whether to sing, cry, scream or shout.

So she did all four.

"What the fuck?" Christine cocked her ears and listened in disbelief. She could hear the sexual noises coming from her neighbour's apartment. She stood by her bedroom door with the bottle of body crème in her hands. She had just gotten out of the shower and was about to lather herself when she heard the passionate cries.

Oh God! Ahhhhhhhh! Ohhhhhhh! Fuckkkkkkk!

It was almost comical. The girl sounded like she was interpreting her orgasm in song.

Ugghh! Ughhhh! Ughh!

Her grunts were inhumane.

Christine licked her lips. He was really putting a hurting on her. Sweet Jesus. The girl sounded as though she was in another world. She could almost see him thrusting inside her with hard, deliberate strokes every time she heard the girl grunt.

She started touching herself without even realizing what she was doing.

Jesus Christ! Hurry up an' come Bambino! Mi can't tek it nuh more! Wait! Wait! Don't stop! I'm coming again! Fuccc-ckkckkkk!

She was coming again. Christine's right hand was a blur as she rubbed her engorged clit ferociously.

She climaxed just as Miranda came inside the house.

"Christine you hear that next door?" she asked as she threw her key down on the kitchen counter and walked over to Christine's bedroom.

Her mouth was a wide O as Christine's shivering naked body greeted her at the bedroom door.

Bambino pulled out and Antoinette crumbled to the floor. He joined her down there and held her legs way back and re-entered her. Antoinette was delirious. She had no idea where the pain stopped and the pleasure started. All she knew was that her head was spinning and she was hurting yet feeling so fucking *good* at the same time. Bambino didn't just have a ridiculously huge dick; he knew how to use to it. She could feel another one coming. But this time it felt like it was miles away, approaching slowly but steadily. It was going to be a big one. Bigger than the gigantic one that had made her hoarse by the time it had subsided.

This was an incredible experience.

A guy she met mere hours ago.

Giving her the fuck of her life.

An encounter that would leave an indelible mark.

On her psyche and her pussy.

Chapter 18

"Oh my God!" Miranda squealed. She couldn't believe that she had caught Christine masturbating to the sounds coming from next door. They both froze before Christine ran into her room and wrapped herself in a towel.

She came back out grinning sheepishly.

"Don't ask," she said heading into the bathroom to wash her hands. "I have no idea what came over me."

Miranda was laughing so hard that Christine had no choice but to join in. Miranda rolled on the floor. Christine sighed as her laugh died down to a chuckle. Miranda was not going to let her live this down for a long time; if ever. Miranda laughed until she had a headache. It was, undoubtedly, the funniest thing she had seen in a very long time.

After taking a shower to freshen up before going home to her boyfriend, Bambino gave Antoinette a ride home. She asked him to drop her off at the entrance of the street that she lived on. She would walk the rest of the way home. Her boyfriend, a bearer for a publishing company, was very jealous and was most likely hanging out with his boys in front of Percy's Pub, where he usually stopped on his way home from work. She had already planned to tell him that her period had come suddenly the moment she saw him so that he wouldn't have sex on his mind later on. It was impossible for her to have sex again tonight or for the next few days. She was feeling so sore and tender down there that it would hurt if he even looked at it. She told Bambino good night and headed down the street. She grimaced as she walked gingerly but she had no regrets. She would do it all over again if given the chance.

Peanuts was not pleased about the developments in Rosewater Meadows. How the fuck was he going to get his cocaine back now that Birdman was dead? He didn't give a shit about any of them dying but he wanted his drugs. The two parcels were worth a lot of money and with a global recession going on, he could not afford to write off such a huge loss. But there was a glimmer of hope. His source in the community had just told him that Bambino had survived because he had not been at the house with the gang and the last time that anyone had seen him was a couple of hours before the shootout when he had ridden out of Rosewater Meadows with a bag strapped to his motorcycle. His source said it appeared as though he was being chased by members of the gang but had gotten away. Very interesting. Peanuts was willing to bet that Bambino had been the one to come over Spanish Town and commit the murder and robbery. He was also willing to bet that the bag Bambino had been seen with contained his precious cocaine. Bambino had to be found. He would use his underground contacts and try to locate him but if that didn't work, he would involve his police friend. The police knew that the gun used to commit the murder in Spanish Town was the same gun used in the slaying of a young woman in Kingston the same morning. They just didn't know the identity of the shooter. He would snitch on Bambino and then when they locked him up; his cronies would get to him in jail and torture him to find out what had happened to the cocaine.

Three days.

If Bambino wasn't found in three days that's the route he would take.

Marcel Chang smiled as he puffed on his cigar. The rich tobacco scent from the imported Cuban cigar permeated the warehouse. He was there along with Corporal Crooks, his gangster friend Matrix and three other cops who had just finishing loading the 500 lbs of marijuana into the warehouse. When Crooks had come by his home precisely at 7, they had a drink and he paid Crooks, who turned out to be a very shrewd negotiator, two hundred thousand dollars; one hundred more than he had intended to pay. Crooks reasoning was that the situation had changed and new people had to be involved to make the deal go through so more money was needed. He didn't quarrel. He paid it. He had gotten back half of his merchandise and his kidnappers were all dead.

Except for one.

"What happened to the one called Bambino?" Chang had asked as they were leaving his home to head down to the warehouse.

"He wasn't at the house," Crooks had replied. "We can find him for you...but it will cost you."

"One hundred thousand dollars if you bring him to me alive," Chang told him. "Fifty if you just kill him and return my Rolex watch. It's very special to me. First luxury item I bought when I became a wealthy man."

"Fifty kinda low man," Crooks had countered.

"Bambino is a known criminal and *should* be a wanted man. Fifty thousand dollars to do your job? Sounds like a good bonus to me," Chang had told him firmly.

And that had been that.

They wrapped up things at the warehouse and everyone went their separate ways. Matrix, a Kirk Lane enforcer, was feeling really upbeat about what was happening. As soon as the cops relaxed their presence in Rosewater Meadows, the Kirk Lane gang would be moving in to take over. With the seasoned gang members dead and the others shell-shocked and disorganized, who was there to stop them? Only Bambino was of any consequence and he was a dead man walking. They would turn Rosewater Meadows into a stronghold for the political party that they supported. That would be a lot of votes as Rosewater was a large, densely populated community. Could be enough to change the West Kingston political landscape. The political spoils, financial and otherwise, that they would receive for delivering Rosewater Meadows to the party, would be substantial. Much talk had been made in recent time about the dismantling of garrisons to curb political tribalism and crime but that's all it was. Talk. The garrisons would be around forever; certain things would never change. And truth be told, the politicians had no real desire to see it change. All they cared about was getting elected and being in power by any means necessary. And the garrisons played the biggest role in the outcome of every general election.

Some very interesting days were ahead.

"I really wished I could have seen you before I left innit," Nisha was saying. She was in the departure lounge at the Norman Manley International Airport. Her flight to London was leaving in two hours. She had managed to get out of Rosewater Meadows and make her way to the airport. She had found three thousand pounds and fifteen hundred euros in a bag in Queenie's closet. "Please don't change your number Bambino...I would like to come back and see you yeah."

"Mi glad seh yuh get out ok," Bambino said sincerely. He rather liked Nisha. She was cool, wasn't a bitch like her half-sister Queenie. And despite her propensity for the gangster life, there was an innocence about her that appealed to him. "Mi number nah change man...nuh worry yuhself."

"I reckon you'll be going back to Rosewater Meadows to take control soon...I want to come back and be right by your side Bambino. I fancy you a great deal," Nisha told him. She was sitting on a chair with her legs crossed, ignoring the leering from a group of three guys seated a few chairs away. She had been through a lot over the past two days. Seeing her sister dead on the floor and her narrow escape from death had rattled her but her thirst for the fast life remained intact nevertheless. And if she was Bambino's girl – his ride and die chick – she would be the happiest girl on earth. England was cool but being in Jamaica and rolling with Bambino was what she wanted. She loved the excitement and the danger. And most of all, she loved Bambino. She had really liked him the first time she saw him and though he never paid her any attention because of Birdman, her strong liking for him had never abated. And now that she had fucked him, sweet Jesus. She could not stop thinking about him.

Bambino smiled to himself. Well, he was open to the idea. Nisha was someone he could trust. It wouldn't hurt to have her in his corner once things got back to normal.

"We'll see babygirl...jus' gwaan chill until t'ings get back to normal," he replied.

He told her to have a safe flight and she promised to call him as soon as possible. Nisha hung up feeling sad. She would have given anything to hear Bambino tell her to miss the flight as he was coming to get her. No such luck though, she would have to wait before she could see him again. She prayed that it wouldn't be too long.

Christine was restless. She was extremely horny. Hearing the guy next door having sex and her subsequent masturbation, had left her in an uncontrollable heat. After locking herself in her bedroom to escape Miranda's mocking laughter, she had tried to watch T.V. but could not concentrate. The ache between her legs was graduating from uncomfortable to being downright painful. She sighed and picked up the phone. She decided to call Clive. Despite his fucked up behaviour over the past few days, tonight was his lucky night. Besides, there was no sex like make-up sex. Maybe this would help them to get back on track. Wasn't it sex or the lack of it that had started the problem in the first place? Though she still had a bitter taste in her mouth from his handling of the situation, she called him nevertheless. Desperate times called for desperate measures. She was going to go stark, raving mad if she didn't get some dick within the hour.

Clive wasn't answering his phone. She redialed. Rang out to voicemail again. That was odd. It was a Wednesday night. Usually, on a Wednesday, if they weren't together,

Clive would be at home chilling as he had to go to work extra early on Thursdays. She checked the time. It was only 8:30. She doubted that he had gone to bed already. She called his land line. Still no response.

Ten minutes later, wearing only a large T-shirt as she planned to jump his bones the minute he opened the door, she headed out to Clive's home. She just *had* to get some dick tonight.

Bambino went straight home after dropping off Antoinette. That had been a good one. He was now feeling relaxed and sated. He tried on a couple of the outfits that he had bought. He was pleased with his purchases. Everything had totaled forty-five thousand dollars. He had enough gear for the upcoming holidays. Christmas was only three weeks away. Depending on what he planned to do New Year's Eve, he might have to get something for that night but that was about it. He went into the living room and sat on the plush leather couch. Reminded him of the one he had at home. This one was a deep burgundy though. He turned the T.V. on and settled on Fox Soccer Channel. He rolled a marijuana joint as he looked at the goals of the month in the English Premier League. He was in a reflective mood. An approaching new year tended to have that effect on people and he was no different. This year had been good. He had made a good amount of money and his reputation had grown by leaps and bounds.

2009 would be even better. He was going to be the don of Rosewater Meadows. He was going to do what Birdman had failed to do: take over Kirk Lane. Fuck the peace treaty. He was going to recruit new gang members, implement strict rules and guidelines for the gang and turn it into a well-oiled efficiently run organization. He had plans for the community too. He wanted a good football team made up of the youths from the community to eventually make it to the island's top tier league. There were a lot of talented footballers in Roswewater Meadows just wasting their talent. He wouldn't leave out the women either. He sometimes passed them playing netball and they seemed to be pretty good. He would also refurbish the community center and do some additions, making it a real place where the residents could hang out and play sports or just chill and listen to some music. The Member of Parliament for the area had made his usual promises but once the votes were delivered and he won back his seat, it was business as usual. He was going to change that. He was going to meet with the MP at least a year and a half before the next election and inform him that if he didn't get certain projects underway in the community immediately, he could kiss his seat goodbye.

He was surprising himself with the thoughts that were invading his head. Thinking like this was alien to him. He couldn't pin point exactly when he had first felt a subtle change coming over him but there was no doubt about it; he was becoming a more rounded person. He chuckled at the revelation.

Mr. I-Don't-Give-A-Fuck-About-Anything actually did.

Christine arrived at Clive's house in twenty minutes. He lived in Mona Commons in the Liguanea area in a nice two bedroom home that his grandfather on his mother's side had willed to him. He had refurbished it and it was now one of the best looking houses on his street. The others weren't too shabby either; it was a decent middle-class neighbourhood.

His ultra fast, fire-engine red Subaru Imprezza was visible in the grilled garage. That meant he was home. A black Honda Accord coupe was parked in the yard. That meant he had company. Christine parked and got out of the vehicle. She made her way into the yard and was about to call out Clive's name when she realized that somebody else was already doing so.

Loudly.

Passionately.

For the second time in less than three hours she was overhearing people having sex.

But this time it was her man.

And she wasn't the one calling out his name.

Chapter 19

"Clive! Clive! Argghhh!" Gina shouted as she climaxed again. Her third. In the past half an hour. Clive always knew how to hit her spots. And tonight it felt like he had discovered a couple more. He was fucking her so good she would suck his daddy's dick. "Clive don't make come again! Please! I can't take another one! Blood-claat! Clive! Yuh never hear mi! Ohhhhh!"

Christine's feet seemed to move by their own accord as she made her way to the side of the house. His bedroom window was open. Her heartbeat sounded even louder in her ears than the girl's proclamation that she didn't want to come again. Imagine that. *Her* man was putting it on this girl so good that she was begging him not to make her come again. You go boy. She tip toed and pushed her hand through the grill and shifted the curtain a bit.

The action was riveting.

The scene was heartbreaking.

A woman watching the man she was with fucking another woman behind her back, without a condom no less, had to be one of the most hurtful things she could ever see in her life.

She watched the expression on his face.

He looked possessed.

She sounded possessed.

He was sweating like a slave.

She was wailing like a banshee.

She couldn't see the girl's face but she could see his thick shaft moving in and out of the woman with wild abandon.

She couldn't watch anymore.

She walked away and got inside her car.

She didn't have the physical strength or the mental fortitude to confront him right now.

She started her car and drove away.

But not before she heard the woman screaming that she wanted him to come all over her face.

Jesus Christ.

Bambino, feeling hungry and wondering why he hadn't gotten some snacks when he was on the road earlier, got dressed in a Ralph Lauren tank top, Evisu shorts and a pair of all white Air Force ones and exited the house. He planned on going to the 24 hour Mini Mart at the Texaco gas station in Half-Way-Tree. The marijuana had given him a serious case of the munchies. His neighbour drove up just as he was closing his front door. He looked over at her before getting on his bike. She got out of the car and leaned against it. She sounded like she was crying. He wasn't even sure if she had realized that he was standing there. He wasn't sure what made him go over there but he did. He walked over and stood in front of her.

She looked up at him through tear-filled eyes.

Whatever had happened had hurt her deeply.

The pain was etched all over her attractive features.

He handed her a rag from his pocket.

She wiped her face and blew her nose.

"Thanks," she murmured, suddenly remembering that she only had on a T-shirt. It was obvious that she didn't have on a bra but he probably thought that she had on shorts or a pair of tights underneath the long T-shirt. His nearness made her nervous. She cleared her throat, thankful that the tears had stopped. This was kind of embarrassing.

They looked at each other for a moment.

"Yuh want to go for a ride?" Bambino asked.

Christine didn't know what she had expected him to say but it wasn't that. Caught her off guard. She loved bikes. She liked him. And she could use a distraction. Why not?

Because you don't know this guy Christine. Suppose he took you somewhere and raped and killed you? Anything could happen. Exercise some good judgment. Tell him thanks but no thanks.

"Give me a minute to change," Christine replied and went inside to clean up her face and slip into something sexy.

She was feeling a little better already.

Fuck good judgement.

Deidre was at the weekly Wednesday night party with her cousin and the girls when her bladder started complaining. She told them that she would soon be back and headed to the bathroom. Matrix watched her as he sipped his Hennessy and red bull from a plastic cup. The gangsters from Kirk Lane were out in full force. They were in a celebratory mood. There were a lot of things to celebrate: the death of Birdman and most of the core members of his crew; their inevitable takeover of Rosewater Meadows and Tech Nyne, the pride and joy of Kirk Lane, had scored another hit song which had entered the billboard charts at #98. It was the first hardcore dancehall song to make it onto the billboard charts. Things were definitely looking up for Kirk Lane in more ways than one. He had been noticing Deidre for several weeks now. But she was from Rosewater Meadows and though there was a truce between the two communities, if he had approached her it would have caused a problem. There was an unspoken rule: the women from both communities were to stick to their own. But things had changed now. He didn't even see any gangster of significance from Rosewater Meadows at the party. He could do whatever the fuck he wanted. And he wanted Deidre.

He walked over to the bathroom and waited by the entrance.

He grabbed her arm as she walked by a few minutes later.

"Ah me name Matrix," he told her, holding on to her arm tightly. "Top shotta from Kirk Lane."

Deidre's arm was hurting but she didn't struggle or show any sign that she was in pain. Though she hadn't been living in Rosewater Meadows for long, she knew the rules and was fiercely loyal to her community. Two days ago this could *never* have happened. But today was a new day, and until Bambino returned and put things back in order – and she was certain he would – they were fair game. She looked at him frostily. She didn't respond.

"We ah go tek over Rosewater Meadows real soon an' ah yuh mi want as mi new piece," he declared with an evil grin. He released her arm and grabbed her right ass cheek. He squeezed it and nodded approvingly. "Yuh sexy nuh bumboclaat enuh gal."

She swallowed a retort but removed his hand from her ass.

"Mi friend dem ah wait pon mi," she told him and walked away quickly.

Matrix watched her as she stood next to her cousin and whispered in her ear. He had gotten an erection just from groping her ass. He couldn't wait to get a hold of her.

Show her what the men of Kirk Lane were made of.

Bambino was sitting on his bike directly in front of her apartment when Christine came back outside ten minutes later. She had put on a little bit of make-up and had slipped into a pair of extremely short Juicy Couture denim shorts, a white baby T and a cute pair of Loeffler Randall sandals. She couldn't see Bambino's face as he was already wearing his helmet but his head was turned in her direction. She climbed onto the bike and Bambino revved the engine loudly before taking off. A vehicle was entering the complex so he didn't need to stop at the gate. Christine hugged him around the waist as he headed out of Havendale and onto Mannings Hill road. It was exciting being on the bike with Bambino. It was a beautiful hunk of metal and chrome and it was as fast as a rocket. She hugged him tightly as Bambino zipped past everything in front of them, including other bikes. Her heart skipped a beat when she felt the object in his waist. He had a gun. She wondered, no hoped it was a licensed firearm. Something told her it wasn't. What if they were pulled over by the cops and he was searched? Who was this guy really? She was scared but intrigued. She couldn't believe it when the bike came to a stop. They had arrived in Half-Way-Tree. In less than ten minutes. Unfuckingbelievable.

Chapter 20

Bambino smiled inwardly as they dismounted. He knew she had felt his gun and probably had a million questions swirling around in her cute little head. They walked into the mini mart and Bambino purchased a huge bag of potato chips, a hot dog, a chicken sandwich and a large bottle of fruit punch. Christine only wanted a snicker bar.

Christine was confused. Here she was, on the road with someone she knew nothing about, he had a gun – an unlicensed gun she was sure, they didn't even know each other's name, and yet, instead of chastising herself for embarking on such a risky excursion, and removing herself from a potentially dangerous situation, she was inexplicably feeling excited and thoroughly enjoying his company. What was it about wholesome, well-brought up girls being attracted to bad boys? It was a phenomenon that warranted an in depth study.

"Yuh enjoy de ride?" he asked as they headed back outside.

"It was exhilarating. I couldn't believe that we got here so quickly. You can really ride," she replied. That had been only the second time he had spoken. He was so quiet it was almost unnerving. She was used to guys going on and on about whatever and showering her with compliments. He was doing none of that. And she knew it wasn't shyness. He was just *different*. She was comfortable though and was amused at the pang of jealousy she had felt when she noticed the cashier smiling seductively at him as he paid for the items. She tried to guess his age but wasn't sure. He looked very young in his face but his manner and demeanour was that of a self-assured, confident man who lived life on his own terms.

Bambino climbed onto the motorcycle, placed the tightly tied bag in front of him, and gunned the engine. He looked around at her when he realized that she was still standing there.

He flicked up the visor on his helmet and looked at her questioningly.

"I refuse to get back onto this motorcycle without us being properly introduced," Christine said with her arms folded.

Bambino chuckled.

He removed his helmet.

He pulled Christine to him abruptly.

She gasped in surprised and he kissed her, slipping his tongue inside her open mouth. He ended the brief but erotic kiss by tugging on her bottom lip.

Christine felt weak. She swooned against him. She couldn't believe he had just done that! In public no less. This guy was so unpredictable.

"Mi name Bambino, you?"

"Christine," she responded, wondering why she was whispering.

"Ok, now get on the bike."

She wondered if Bambino had somehow hypnotized her. Everything he said or did turned her on. How the hell could he talk to her like that and have her like it?

He was a sorcerer. An obeah man or something. There was no other explanation. In a daze, she got onto the bike and they headed out. She screamed and hugged him tightly as he popped a wheelie on Eastwood Park Road. She swore that her heart had jumped out of her chest. Bambino was so crazy. What kind of name was that anyway? She smiled in his back as the motorcycle roared onto Red Hills Road. She was having so much fun that her heartbreaking discovery a mere hour ago had retreated to the back of her mind – at least for now.

Corporal Crooks rubbed his pimple-riddled jaw as he hung up the phone. His contacts at the airport had not seen Bambino. He had emailed a photograph to his counterpart who worked in the departure lounge for him to quietly find out if Bambino had been seen. It would have been so much easier if he could have issued an all points bulletin but the search for Bambino was unofficial. This was a personal matter. The money for his capture was low but he wanted to stay on Marcel Chang's good side and besides, in these harsh economic times and with Christmas right around the corner, the fifty thousand dollars was nothing to scoff at. He had visited Rosewater Meadows today and roughed up a few people but no one seemed to know where Bambino was. He simply had not been seen in the past two days and had not been spotted at any of his usual hang out spots. He had not left the island. He was not known to have any relatives in any of the rural parishes so most likely he was still in Kingston. So where the fuck was he hiding? For someone who stood out in a crowd and rode a distinguishable motorcycle, Bambino was proving to be as slippery as an eel.

Peanuts was not pleased that Bambino had not been found yet. Though he was willing to allow his soldiers to search for three days, he was getting impatient. The three girls who were supposed to transport some of the cocaine to the United States were ready to go. His money was being tied up and he didn't like that. It was like Bambino had vanished into thin air. The only positive news he had heard was that a bike resembling Bambino's had been seen in Half-Way-Tree last night in the vicinity of the 24 hour Texaco gas station. Wasn't much but it was a start. They would increase their vigilance in that area and hope for the best.

Bambino pulled up in front of his apartment and parked the motorcycle.

Christine watched him as he removed his helmet. *He's so fucking handsome. Real man candy. And those lips. God!*

"Thanks for the ride," Christine began, trying to convince herself that she was going to say goodnight now and go inside the safety of her apartment where she wouldn't be tempted to do something she had never done before. "I enjoyed it. You did a good job of cheering me up."

Bambino looked at her with a stoic expression. He didn't respond.

When it was apparent that he wasn't going to say anything, she decided it was best to just go.

"Ok goodnight Bambino...I'll see you around," she told him, expecting her legs to start moving. But they didn't. It was as though she was rooted to the spot.

"Alright...sleep tight," Bambino finally said.

Christine nodded and her legs finally started to work. She walked away slowly and went inside her apartment. She was surprised to see her cell phone on the bed. She hadn't even realized that she had left it. Eight missed calls and a text message. Six of them had been from Clive. She emitted a mirthless chuckle as the sight of him fucking that girl started playing in her head like it was the movie of the week. Asshole. It was over. She wasn't even going to talk to him about it. She didn't want to hear any bull-shit excuses. And she couldn't deal with the stress. She wasn't about to let anything put her back in that dark depressed state that she had been in after her sister's murder. And that included Clive. Three years. That was a long time to be in relationship. And it had been good for the most part. Ripped apart and destroyed because of sex.

Sex had been the catalyst. First they had argued about the lack of it, and then she had caught him having it. With somebody else.

Please don't make me come again Clive!

Come all over my face Clive!

God it hurts.

Bitch.

Bastard.

Miranda knocked on her bedroom door before opening it and popping her head in.

"You ok Chrissy?" she asked, stifling a yawn. She had been studying nonstop since she got home from work. She went to University part time and had an exam tomorrow evening. She was doing her Masters in Business Administration. Working and going to school was difficult but she had given herself until thirty to achieve certain goals and she only had four years to go so she had to do what she had to do.

Christine nodded and smiled weakly.

Miranda knew that something was wrong but she knew that Christine would talk about it when she was ready.

"Ok see you tomorrow. Going to bed," she replied and closed the door.

Christine undressed, turned off the light and went underneath her comforter.

She was wet.

Had been from the moment she had gotten on the bike with Bambino and wrapped her arms around him.

Had gotten *ridiculously* wet after the kiss.

The only thing that had saved her from not being fucked into next year by him right now was the fact that he hadn't pushed it. If he had actually invited her in it would have been a done deal. She wondered what *that* said about her. She chalked up her close fuck-on-the-first-date call to meeting a really sexy guy that she had been admiring at a time when she was feeling hurt and vulnerable. That's all there was to it.

She sighed and closed her eyes.

It had been a day that she wouldn't soon forget.

Chapter 21

Clive was in a foul mood all day Thursday. Christine had not returned his calls and her mobile was off. He had called her on the office line three times only to be told that she was unable to take a call. What kind of game was Christine playing? He was going to swing by her apartment and find out what the hell was going on. And she had better have a good goddamn excuse for her behaviour. He was tired of her treating him like a punk.

Bambino stayed in all day. Something told him not to go on the road today and he had heeded the voice. He chilled and watched T.V. and slept all day, ordering food to be delivered to him when he was hungry. He had gotten a few calls. Deidre had called to tell him about her run in with a guy named Matrix from Kirk Lane at the weekly Wednesday night party. Bambino knew the punk. Had slept with both his girlfriend and his sister. Bambino had chuckled at his comment that he 'was a walking dead man'. He had told Deidre not to worry as he would be back in a few weeks to sort things out but that if she wanted, she could go back to the country to chill until the New Year. She told him that she would think about doing that as she really didn't want to be at the mercy of Matrix or anyone else from Kirk Lane. She also told him that several policemen had been asking about his whereabouts. He thanked her and told her to take care of herself. He was just about to roll up a marijuana joint when he heard an insistent horn blowing outside his apartment. His dinner of jerk pork, festival and rice and peas ordered from Jerk on Wheels had arrived. He went outside wearing only a pair of Puma sweats and socks and flip flops.

His neighbour, Christine, had just gotten home. A car had driven in right behind her. The guy parked behind Christine's car and hopped out quickly. He then walked over to Christine's car and tried to open the driver's door. It was locked. He banged loudly on the top of the car.

"Christine! Stop the foolishness and come out of the car!" he shouted. "Yuh jus' ah behave like a little child! If you have a problem let us talk about it and stop ignoring me!"

Bambino paid for his food and watched for a few more seconds before going inside. Christine wasn't saying anything but she was crying. Bambino was willing to bet that this punk was the reason that she had been crying yesterday. He took his food inside, placed his desert eagle in his waist, slipped on a shirt, and went back outside. The last thing he needed was to draw attention to himself but Christine seemed as though she needed some assistance.

Christine was still sitting in the car when he got back out there. She looked even more distraught. And embarrassed. The guy had gotten angrier.

"Christine! Are you a fucking idiot? Come out of the fucking car!" he shouted as he used his knuckles to rap on the window loudly.

Bambino walked over to Clive and grabbed him by his shirt.

"Pussyhole! Who the fuck you be? Let mi go!" Clive shouted as he tried to pry Bambino's fingers loose.

Bambino punched him in the face and flung him to the ground. Clive jumped up back up quickly.

"Hey bwoy relax before mi buss yuh skull," Bambino snarled, lifting his shirt slightly so that Clive could see his gun.

Clive froze with a frightened look on his face.

"Jump inna yuh car an' gwaan bout yuh bloodclaat business an' if Christine ever tell me seh yuh badda har again mi ah go find yuh and murder yuh bloodclaat. A me name Bambino. If yuh nuh know the name pussy yuh betta ask somebody."

"A-a-a-alright b-b-boss...just relax...mi ah go leave now...everyt'ing good," Clive stuttered as he hurriedly jumped in his car. The name sounded vaguely familiar but he was too scared to place it now. He reversed and the security guard opened the gate and let him through. He headed down the street confused and frightened. Why was Christine acting like this? Who was that guy? Had she left him for a fucking gangster? Nothing was making any sense. He needed a strong drink. He headed home. There was an unopened bottle of Hennessy in the liquor cabinet. That should do the trick.

Christine was in shock and awe at the series of events that had just taken place. She had been annoyed when she realized that Clive had driven in behind her. Her annoyance had given way to fear when he became belligerent and angry. She had never seen him act like that. Beating on her car and cursing her out and calling her names. It had been scary. Then Bambino had come out and kicked Clive's ass as easily as he would take a stroll across the street. He had seen that she was in trouble and had defended her without a second thought. He barely even knew her. She realized that there was no denying that they had a connection. It was inexplicable but it was there. As real and as tangible as the car in which she was sitting. She looked out the window at him. He was standing by the car looking at her with his usual stoic expression.

The epitome of cool.

She wondered if he shit ice cubes.

She opened the door and got out of the car. Her legs felt rubbery. She swayed and Bambino held her. She hugged him tightly.

"Thank you so much…he was just acting so crazy… threatening me…I don't know what would have happened if you hadn't intervened…" she sobbed.

Still holding her, he locked her car door and slipped the keys in her pants pocket. He then walked towards his apartment with his arm around her.

Christine didn't resist or protest. The last two days had been something out of a novel. Suddenly her life was filled with more drama than a James Patterson thriller. They entered his apartment and he locked the door.

"I need to use the bathroom," she said to him. He nodded and released her. All the apartments on this side of the complex had the same design so she knew where to find it.

Christine went inside the bathroom and closed the door. She did number one, wiped and flushed the toilet. She went over to the face basin and examined her tear-stained face as she washed her hands. She had cried so much in the past month and a half. Her sister's murder and now the situation with Clive had caused her to shed many tears. She was tired of crying so much and feeling so sad. The good Lord probably realized that she needed a change. Maybe that's why he sent Bambino in her life. That would explain why it felt so natural being around him. Why she was so attracted and connected to him in such a short space of time. She washed her face with just water – she only used a certain product on her face and of course, Bambino wouldn't have that here. She wanted to take a shower. Bambino wouldn't mind. She pulled the shower curtain back and looked what was available. There was a bar of soap as well as a bottle of shower gel. She stripped down and went in.

Bambino could hear the shower running as he heated up the food that he had ordered in the microwave. It was risky what he had done. He was here to lay low for a little while. Not to get entangled in other people's personal disputes. Yet he had. Without giving it a second thought. Why did he like this girl so much? Why did he care? He didn't have the answers. He was so deep in thought that it was a few moments before he realized that she was calling his name. The microwave beeped as he walked over to the bathroom. The door was slightly cracked. She was attempting to hide her body as she asked him for a towel. He could see her right breast. It was wet, firm and more than a handful. The nipple seemed to be erect. He wondered if the cold water was the cause of that. He doubted it. He went into the bedroom and returned to the bathroom with a plush beige towel. She opened the door just wide enough to receive it. She smiled her thanks and closed the door.

Bambino had shared the food in two plates and poured them two glasses of fruit punch by the time Christine came out of the bathroom.

"Mmmm…that smells delicious," she said as Bambino handed her a tray. "You made this?"

Bambino laughed.

"I'm a gangster not a chef."

Christine looked at him, surprised by his admission. He had said it so casually, so-matter-of-factly, like he was an accountant or a musician. A man at peace with himself. A man who lived by his own rules.

She had been wary and afraid of men like Bambino all her life. Yet here she was falling for one. Sitting in his apartment wearing only a towel, eating some of his dinner that he had shared. Wondering what it was going be like when they made love. Surprised at the ease with which she had accepted the fact that when she left this apartment Bambino would have intimate knowledge of her body. Surprised at how anxious she was for him to have that knowledge. She wondered if he would make her scream and moan at the top of her lungs like that girl yesterday. She sure hoped so. It was as though Bambino had taken control of her senses. He had her in a spell. Just being in his presence was enough to give her butterflies in her stomach and moisture in her special place. His stoic, penetrating gaze made her body feel weak all over. Bambino turned the on the T.V. Sports was on. She watched as they showed highlights from a recent Manchester United game. Christiano Ronaldo had scored a magnificent goal. He was hot. But not as hot as Bambino.

Christine took a bite of the jerk pork. It was good. Really good. Made her realize just how hungry she was. They finished their mostly silent but comfortable, enjoyable meal and took the dishes into the kitchen. Bambino accepted her offer to clean up and when she returned to the living room, he was reclined on the couch smoking a large spliff. She went over there and sat between his legs. He hugged her to him and placed the marijuana joint at her lips. She had smoked cigarettes before when she was in college a few years ago but had never tried weed. She opened up and took a drag. She inhaled the potent marijuana and after three drags, she felt like she was floating.

She turned her head and looked up at Bambino. He exhaled and when the smoke cleared, he lowered his head and claimed her lips.

Chapter 22

The kiss was soft. And gentle. At first. Then Christine cupped the back of his head with her left hand and kissed him deeply, exploring his mouth anxiously, searching and finding the sweet pleasures that were there for her. She moaned in his mouth as she felt him open her towel and caress her aching breasts. Her nipples were so hard they hurt. Bambino placed the marijuana joint in the ashtray and carried Christine in his arms to the bedroom.

He placed her on the bed like she was a delicate, expensive piece of china. He even surprised himself at his gentleness.

He undressed slowly and Christine made a sound that was somewhere between a gasp and a croak when his turgid shaft sprung into view. Her eyes, wide with wonder, went from his dick to his face, then back to his dick. Christine had seen a dick on a porno flick once that was so huge, she had dismissed it as a camera trick. She had thought it impossible for a dick to be that big. This one was bigger. And it wasn't a camera trick. It was right before her very eyes.

Bambino stood by the side of the bed and Christine crawled over to him and touched it. It felt like granite. She cupped his testicles with one hand as she stroked it slowly. They say that seeing is believing but even though she was seeing it and touching it, she was still in disbelief.

She looked up at him, her face a vision of disbelief, wanton desire and fright.

"Bambino...oh God...it's so fucking huge...where are you going put this monstrous thing...huh...it's bigger than you..."

Bambino grabbed a fistful of her hair and directed her head downwards. Her words were turning him on immensely. He wasn't so gentle anymore.

She complied and licked around the bulbous head and tip. She then covered the head with her mouth, wrapping her tongue around it and sucking insistently.

Bambino growled like a provoked lion. She was sucking his dick just the way he liked it. He liked his blow jobs to be sloppy and loud with lots of slurping noises and moans. He liked when a woman looked and sounded like she was enjoying having his dick in her mouth.

By all indications Christine was having a ball. She tried to see how much of it she could take in then released it from mouth as she gasped for air.

"Ahh...so fucking big...taste so fucking good though...feels so powerful..." she murmured breathlessly as she stroked him. She continued to stroke him as she lowered her head and claimed his testicles in her mouth. She sucked them and twirled them around with her tongue, grimacing in sweet pain as Bambino tightened his grip on her hair.

"I'm so wet Bambino...my pussy is dripping...I want you so bad...but I'm so scared...you're going to make me scream and cry with that big dick..."

That did it.

Bambino roared and pushed her on her back and placed her on the edge of the bed. He positioned himself between her legs and Christine, her face etched in anticipation and worry, propped herself on her elbows so she could watch him enter her. A part of her was still dubious that he would be able to actually fit. She realized that he was unsheathed but at that moment, she didn't care. Her eyes were the size of truck tyres as Bambino placed the head at the entrance of her pulsating wetness and slid it in gently.

"Awww...awww...aww...ohhhh...fuck..."

The pain was indescribable.

She felt like she was going to die.

Perspiration flowed from her pores and the veins in her forehead became pronounced. She continued to watch as more and more of his mammoth pole disappeared inside her.

Just when she was going to beg him to stop as the pain had become unbearable, a curious thing happened. His dick touched a spot that felt so good she screamed.

"Fuck! Right. There. Bambino. Right. Fucking. There."

Bambino stroked her slowly with long, measured strokes, hitting the spot over and over again.

"Oh Jesus! I'm going to come Bambino! I'm going to come so fucking hard my heart is going to stop! Its right there Bambino! Bumbopussyrassclaat! Ahhhh! Ahhhh! Ahhhh!"

Bambino moaned as she climaxed all over his throbbing dick. It felt so good. He could literally feel her juices bathing him over and over again. She had climaxed really hard. Her eyes had rolled so far to the back of her head that all he could see were two white spots.

"Mmmm….mmmm…mmmm…mmmm…" Christine moaned as she savoured the most intense orgasm she had ever experienced. She felt like she was having an out of body experience.

Bambino resumed stroking her fire. He increased his tempo. Her pussy was so saturated and felt so *good*; like it was filled and overflowing with warm honey.

From intense pain to intense pleasure.

It had been a dramatic and sudden turnaround.

One minute she felt as though she was going to die from pain, the next minute she was *sure* she had died from pleasure. Bambino had been blessed with a gigantic sugar stick. It had to have been constructed entirely of sugar. It felt so exquisitely sweet. A man should not have such a dick and be able to fuck this good.

It was too much power for one man to have.

Right now he could get her to do or say anything he wanted. *Anything.* That was some scary shit.

"Yes Bambino! Ohhh…you're fucking me so good baby… so fucking good…your big dick is so sweet…feels so good baby…give it to me Bambino!"

Her words had a direct impact on his dick. Impossibly, it seemed to swell even bigger inside her. Another orgasm was on the way. It felt like it was going to be so powerful that Christine was scared. He was fucking her hard now, really punishing her pussy. Hitting spots that were fighting each other for the right to make her climax.

"Oh god! Fuck me! You evil, wicked motherfucker! You want me to die! You're trying to fuck me to death! Ok! Ok! Kill me then! Kill me to rass! I'm coming baby! I'm coming! I'm going to scream this fucking roof off!"

The roof stayed on but she did try her best. It was a blood-curling wail that made those at home in the neighbourhood wonder what the hell was going on.

Bambino struggled to hold back his climax. He wasn't ready yet. He wanted to fuck her doggystyle before he came. He had wanted to do that to her since the first time he laid eyes on her.

When her orgasm subsided, he pulled out and made her stand up, slightly bent over. He then entered her and held her by the wrists as he fucked her mercilessly.

He was fucking her so hard that she was threatening to topple over though he was holding her wrists tightly.

Christine started speaking to the dead.

"Nadine! Woi mi sister come save mi! Bambino is killing me! Rescue me my sister!"

She moved forward and Bambino moved with her, still stroking her like a man fucking to save his life.

It sounded like two animals were in the room.

Bambino finally backed her up in the corner by the closet and released her hands. She placed them on the wall for support as Bambino grunted his way to his impending climax.

"Oh God! You're about to come baby? I feel your big, sweet dick throbbing! Come for me baby! Wet up this fucking pussy! Wet it up!"

Bambino did just that.

"Christine!" he shouted as the climax he had twice delayed gushed from him angrily. "Christine! Christine!"

"Yes baby! Ohhhh! Yes baby! It's your's now baby!"

Bambino's knees wobbled from the intensity of his orgasm.

He hugged Christine tightly as his frame shook like he was having a seizure.

They collapsed to the floor.

Chapter 23

"Bambino? The name sound familiar but mi nuh too sure. I'll call one of my shotta friends and get some information," Everton, one of Clive's more street oriented acquaintances, said. He was a barber by profession but he was from a volatile community and though he didn't live in the ghetto anymore, a lot of his friends still did.

Clive, having had a few drinks and given himself some time to recover from his experience earlier that evening, had called Everton to vent and to see if he knew anything about this gangster who had beaten him up and embarrassed him in front of his woman.

Everton promised to call him back later and hung up. Clive poured himself another drink. He just couldn't understand why Christine was treating him like this. It was her fault why he had gotten beat up. If she had been answering his calls or had come out of the car when he asked her to, none of this would have happened. He wondered if Miranda knew what was going on. He dialed her number.

Miranda was in a taxi heading home when her phone rang. It was Clive. She answered the call.

"Hi Clive," she said.

"Miranda what's up…I need to talk to you about Christine."

She figured as much. They were cool and all but he wouldn't have any reason to be calling her unless it had something to do with Christine.

"Ok, what's up?"

Clive spent the next five minutes complaining about the way Christine had been ignoring him, ending with an edited version of the fight he had with the guy next door.

Miranda was stunned. The guy next door fought Clive over Christine? It just didn't make any sense. Christine didn't even know the guy. And why was she ignoring Clive like that? She knew they were having their problems but it seemed that things had deteriorated rapidly. Obviously she was out of the loop as none of this made any sense to her. She also doubted Clive had told her the whole story. Well, hopefully Christine was home and she would be able to speak to her and find out exactly what was going on.

"I've been busy preparing for my exam today Clive so I really don't know what's going on," Miranda replied.

"Ok well shout me back after you've gotten a chance to talk to her," Clive responded.

Miranda agreed though she planned to do no such thing. She would talk to Christine but for her benefit, not his. She was not going to get caught up in any gossiping about her best friend with Clive. She was thoughtful as she hung up the phone. The security guard opened the gate and the cab entered the complex. He pulled up in front of her home and she paid him and got out.

Christine's car was in the driveway.

Good.

She was home.

Chapter 24

"I can't find the words to describe what just happened," Christine murmured with a contented sigh. They were still on the carpeted floor. Still trying to catch their breath. She ran her manicured fingers through his curly mane. Not only couldn't she articulate just how good and incredible the sex had been; she still couldn't understand how she had slept with Bambino so quickly and easily. She was also stunned by her behaviour during the act. She had been like an animal. She had never felt so loose and free before while having sex. She blushed as she recalled some of the things she had said while Bambino was pounding her into oblivion. Her pussy was still throbbing. It felt like Bambino was still inside her. "You're stuck with me Bambino...you cannot fuck me like that and don't stay in my life."

Bambino chuckled.

Christine pinched his left nipple. "I'm serious though Bambino...I mean things kind of moved at the speed of light but I'm not into casual sex...I'm not asking for a commitment at this point but I'd like to know that I mean something to you and this was not just a fuck."

THE GARRISON

She hoped she wasn't pushing too hard. But she really needed to know that he wouldn't just brush her aside after tonight. She didn't think he would but she *needed* to *know* that he wouldn't. Conventional wisdom would dictate that the last thing she needed was to jump into another relationship so soon but this wasn't a conventional situation. And the comfort and pleasure she got from being with Bambino was exactly what the doctor ordered.

Bambino shifted so he could look at her. They were from two different worlds. Lead completely different lives. Could it even work? They had an insane chemistry but would that be enough? He was also still trying to wrap his head around the fact that he had passionately cried out her name when he climaxed. He had never done that before. She made him feel vulnerable. A feeling he wasn't sure he liked very much. He had grown up not being attached to anything or anyone. There was nothing in his life he couldn't walk away from at the drop of a hat if he needed to. There was no one in his life that anyone could use to get to him. And that suited him just fine. A man in his position couldn't afford emotional attachments. But he liked her very much. No denying that. What to do? There were so many questions but few answers. Well, he didn't plan to make his triumphant return to Rosewater Meadows until after the Christmas holidays. That gave him a couple of weeks to figure things out.

He kissed her.

On the forehead.

Tenderly.

She smiled and hugged him.

She *felt* everything she wanted to hear in that kiss.

Miranda was puzzled, and a tad bit worried, as she dialed Christine's number. Her car was out front and she was nowhere to be seen. Had Clive done something to her and was trying to cover his tracks by calling her to speak about Christine? It wasn't farfetched. These were serious times. Anything could happen to anyone these days. If Christine didn't answer her phone, she would call the police.

Christine picked up on the fourth ring.

"Chrissy! Are you ok? Where are you?"

Christine chuckled. "I've never been better...I'm next door."

Miranda bristled. Here she was being concerned and Christine was next door frolicking with the new neighbour.

"I see...well I just wanted to know that you are ok. Clive had called me saying some things and when I got home and saw your car but didn't see you I kind of got worried. What is going on Christine?"

Christine smiled to herself. Her best friend called her Christine only when she was pissed at her. Miranda was feeling left out.

"We'll talk about everything soon hun," Christine said soothingly. "A lot has happened in a short space of time so I haven't really gotten a chance to even digest everything yet much less to talk to you about it."

"Ok, well no matter what time you come over please wake me up," Miranda responded.

Christine glanced at the thick python between Bambino's legs resting on the carpet. It was flaccid but was almost to his knees. Sweet Jesus. She licked her lips.

"Umm...I don't think I'll see you until you come in from work tomorrow," Christine told her.

Miranda was incredulous.

"So you're not going to work tomorrow?"

"No I'm going to call in sick," Christine replied chirpily. She hadn't thought of it until she actually uttered the words and though she wasn't used to being spontaneous, it felt good. What was Bambino doing to her? Fucking obeah man.

Miranda was perturbed about Christine's behaviour. She obviously was not reacting well to whatever had happened between her and Clive. Fucking a guy that she barely knew? Sleeping out? Skipping work? That was not Christine.

"Ok Christine, guess I'll talk to you whenever then," Miranda said frostily.

"Bye hun." Christine was all smiles when she hung up the phone. She was on a high and not even Miranda acting like a mother hen could get her down. It was the first time since her sister's murder that she actually felt happy.

And she owed it all to the handsome, ridiculously well-endowed man lying in her lap.

Chapter 25

"**B**ambino? Yeah man, 'im come from Rosewater Meadows," the youth, known as Predator for obvious reasons, said as he took a swig from the bottle of beer that he was drinking. He was on the corner hanging out in a section of Gravel Hill, an inner-city community located in the Three Miles area of downtown Kingston, when his friend Everton had called to enquire if he knew a gangster by the name of Bambino. "Ah wah happen?"

"Bambino beat up one ah mi brethren," Everton told him.

The youth chuckled. "Him lucky seh ah only beat up 'im get. Bambino is a man weh mek 'im gun do de talking."

They chatted for awhile longer before Everton told him that he would be passing through the area on Sunday and would link him up then and ended the call.

Everton then called back Clive to let him know what he had found out.

A tall, scraggly almost emaciated man slinked away from the corner and took out his cell phone to make a call.

Today was his lucky day. He had been in the right place at the right time. He had overheard Predator's conversation. Whoever had called him had asked about Bambino. Apparently Bambino had beat up somebody that the caller knew. It must have been recently. Corporal Crooks had called him yesterday asking if he had seen Bambino in the area or knew of anyone who had seen him recently. The man, Bones, was an informer for the police. He received money anytime he gave them useful information. He didn't know where Bambino was but by telling them about Predator's conversation, all they had to do was get Predator to tell them who had called him asking about Bambino and take it from there. It seems Bambino was in demand. Word on the street was that Peanuts, the respected don from Spanish Town, was also looking for him. But Bones knew which side his bread was buttered. Corporal Crooks always looked out for him so that's who he would give this bit of potentially important information.

Corporal Crooks answered on the first ring.

"Thank you," Christine whispered as she kissed his smooth jaw. They had finally gotten up from off the floor and were now curled up on the plush leather sofa watching T.V. The video for M.I.A.'s hit song *Paper Planes* was on. Christine loved her music and style. She was just different.

Bambino looked at her questioningly.

"For making me feel so happy," she explained with a smile. "I haven't felt such unadulterated joy since my sister was murdered."

"Sorry to hear dat...how did it happen?" Bambino responded.

"Yeah...I'm still not really over it...probably never will get over it but I'm dealing with it much better now. She was killed a little over a month ago. Fatally shot in a car-jacking incident."

Bambino's heart rate accelerated.

Oh shit. Now he knew why Christine had looked so familiar when he had first seen her.

The girl he had killed was her sister!

He could see her now. Her attractive face, made less so by her acne problem, tight with fear.

For the first time in his young life, he regretted killing somebody.

Corporal Crooks moved quickly after getting the call from Bones. He finally had something to go on. He got to Gravel Hill at 9:30 p.m. in an unmarked police car with two of his closest friends from the Special Crimes Unit. He went to the corner where Bones had told him that he could find Predator. Sure enough, he was there. He was sitting on a crate, smoking a marijuana joint while he watched some of his friends play a game of dominoes.

Corporal Crooks sped up and then braked suddenly in front of the group of men. They jumped up and became wary as it could have been a drive by. He hopped out with his gun drawn and walked over to the men. The other two cops who accompanied him stayed in the car but had their windows down with their guns ready.

"Hey ugly bwoy! Come here!" Crooks disrespectfully addressed Predator.

Predator scowled and apparently taking too long to move for Crooks' liking, was unceremoniously pulled from off of the crate by his shirt and treated to a hard back-handed slap.

"Weh dat fah? Mi jus' deh yah chill and yuh come box mi inna mi face fi no fuckin' reason!" Predator protested angrily. The only thing he hated more than a cop were two cops. All they were good for was to come into the ghetto and brutalize the youths. Treat them like animals, like they didn't have any rights just because they lived in the slums.

Corporal Crooks hit him again.

This time with his firearm.

Blood flowed from Predator's busted mouth.

The men from the community started to defend Predator.

Shouts of 'Low de youth!' and 'Pussyhole babylon' made the other two cops exit the car and train their guns on the growing mob.

"Go inside the car! I'm arresting you for possession of marijuana," Corporal Crooks said as he hauled Predator and flung him onto the backseat.

The other two cops kept their guns pointed at the crowd as they cautiously went into the car and sped away.

They had to be careful as sometimes, gangsters from these communities did not hesitate to open fire on the police.

Corporal Crooks headed down to Marcus Garvey Boulevard and turned off on a road that during the day-time teemed with activity as it housed several large ware-houses, and trailers and trucks carrying goods went in and out for most of the day, but at this time of the night, the place was deserted. Not even a fly would be caught dead in these parts after dark. He pulled over to the side of the road and got out.

Predator, who had been placed between the two cops in the back of the car, was kicked to the ground.

Corporal Crooks placed the nozzle of his gun on the back of Predator's head.

"Ugly bwoy...where is Bambino?" he asked.

Predator was surprised and a bit confused by the question. Why would they be asking him for Bambino? He knew the guy, yes, everyone did, but Bambino didn't frequent Gravel Hill so why would they think that he knew where he was?

"How mi fi know?" Predator responded.

"Hey bwoy...yuh wah dead tonight?" Corporal Crooks growled as he pressed the gun down hard. "Yuh neva deh pon de phone today ah talk to somebody about Bambino?"

Predator thought for a few moments. Then he remem-bered. Everton had called him asking about Bambino. But who could have told the cops about the harmless conversa-tion?

Predator was no snitch but he'd be damned if he was going to die over something as simple as this. He explained the nature of the phone call and told them where they could find Everton.

Satisfied that he had gotten all of the information that Predator could possibly provide, Corporal Crooks hopped into the car and they drove off, leaving Predator on the ground.

Predator got up from off of the ground and brushed himself off. He touched his mouth and winced. His bottom lip was swollen. He didn't have a dollar in his pocket to catch a bus or cab so he would have to walk home. He cursed Crooks and every cop in the police force as he made his way quickly out to Marcus Garvey Boulevard. He wasn't safe here. An exiled gangster from Gravel Hill was the leader of a gang that operated close to this area. He would be killed on sight if they spotted him.

His thoughts were on the informer in the camp as he kept an eye out for his enemies. He would have to warn the men who hung out on the corner to be extra careful. The informer would eventually be found and killed.

And his death would not be a quick one.

Chapter 26

"**B**abes...wake up," Bambino said as he nudged Christine gently. They had fallen asleep on the couch watching the new James Bond flick *Quantum of Solace* on Cinemax. The movie was good but fatigue had kicked in and they had both drifted off into slumber land.

"Hmmm..." Christine moaned sleepily as she stirred.

"Bed time," Bambino told her and they got up from off the couch. Bambino turned off the T.V. and she held his hand as they made their way to the bedroom in the semi-darkness.

They climbed into bed and snuggled up underneath the comforter. They spooned with Christine's back to Bambino. Her warm nude body woke his dick from its slumber.

It sprang to life.

Christine felt the sudden, heavy movement.

Sleep retreated and she moaned loudly and as Bambino slowly slid his dick inside her. She was already wet, as though her pussy had been anticipating this late night pleasure snack. Bambino hugged her tightly as he moved his waistline in a slow, circular motion.

He had felt unsettled when he had initially woken up. He had dreamt about a wedding. That usually meant death. He rarely ever remembered his dreams yet this one was crystal clear when he woke up.

Christine reached around and squeezed his thigh painfully as she climaxed.

"Mmmm…Bambino…mmmm…you make me come so fast…you own this pussy…" Christine breathed.

She loved the way he was fucking her: nice and slow. When he fucked her like this it enabled her to feel every delightful inch of his massive tool in a different but no less pleasant way than when he handled her roughly.

The first time they had *fucked*.

This time they were making love.

She loved the way how Bambino was hugging her tightly and planting soft, sweet kisses on her neck and ear.

She felt so needed.

Desired.

Loved.

He probably wouldn't admit it anytime soon but she knew he loved her.

And she him.

Love at first sight.

Or more like love at first fuck.

Two days ago she would've thought all of this would have been impossible.

She was now a former cynic.

Bambino had turned her into a true believer.

Chapter 27

The following morning, Clive was about to reverse out of his driveway when he realized that a car was parked in front of his gate, blocking him. He blew his horn insistently but the tinted car did not move. He hopped out of his car angrily and walked over to the car. He rapped on the window on the driver's side.

The window came down slowly and the nozzle of a 9mm pistol told him good morning. His eyes widened in shock and his knees buckled in fear.

Jesus Christ! Bambino hear seh mi ah ask question 'bout him an' him track mi down fi kill mi!

"I'm not going to hurt you…I'm a police officer…I just need some information. Get in the back," Corporal Crooks told him. He had found Everton early this morning. He wasn't home when they went there to look for him so they had staked out his home all night. He had finally shown up at 6:30 a.m. He had gone to a weekly street dance that unbelievably just really got going at sunrise. Their interrogation had led them to this fellow, Clive, who had been beaten up by Bambino over the guy's girlfriend. Corporal Crooks was tired but he wanted the one hundred thousand dollars and the chance to build goodwill with Marcel Chang. Show him that he could get the job done; no matter what it was. Hopefully after this his next stop would be wherever Bambino was hiding out.

Clive did as he was told; praying that what the man had just said was true. He would tell them whatever they needed to know so that they wouldn't have any reason to hurt him.

"Tell me what happened between you and the man called Bambino," Corporal Crooks said, looking around at him with his bloodshot sleep-deprived eyes.

Clive told him about the fight.

Corporal Crooks smiled.

The search was over.

Hopefully he would be able to capture Bambino alive. Dead, he would be only worth half of the hundred thousand.

"Give me the address," Corporal Crooks said triumphantly.

Clive told him.

"Ok, get out and have a nice day."

He didn't have to be told twice. He hopped out and watched as the car sped off. It was a few minutes before his breathing became normal again. He got in his car and headed out to work. He wasn't even going to call Everton and ask him if he was the one that had sent the cops to him. He wanted to know nothing. They had left him alone and that was all that mattered. Matter of fact, he would never speak to Everton again. Being a shown a gun in a threatening manner twice in less than twenty four hours had really rattled him. He didn't feel safe. He decided to put in for his vacation. A two week trip to New York to spend some time with his cousins sounded really good right about now.

God knows he needed a break from all this drama.

"Why are you up so early babes?" Christine asked, as she sat up in bed. The sheet fell away, exposing her full breasts. She yawned and smiled at Bambino. He returned her smile but his eyes looked serious; like something was on his mind.

"Mi feel like go fi ah ride...and mi ah go buy us some breakfast," he replied.

"Ok baby, don't stay too long."

She looked at the time. Almost 7 a.m. She would take a shower and then call the office to let them know that she wouldn't be coming in.

Bambino nodded and exited the bedroom.

She heard the front door open and close, followed by the roar of his motorcycle as he headed out of the complex.

Christine got up and went inside the bathroom to take a shower.

Bambino was a troubled man.

First the dream, now the *feeling*.

He was having that feeling again. He rode all the way to Lookout Point in Red Hills. It was a popular hang out spot where people would go to chill and enjoy the magnificent view at night. It was empty now. He parked the motorcycle and sat on a rock. He rolled a small marijuana joint and lit it. He inhaled deeply. His mind was all over the place. He wondered what was happening on the streets. He had been laying low for only two days but it felt like two months.

He wondered if Nisha was ok. He wondered if Deidre had taken his advice and was now in the country. He wondered if he was making a mistake by planning to stay away from Rosewater Meadows until the New Year. The danger of the men from Kirk Lane moving in to take advantage of the relatively defenseless community was a real one. Who was there to defend the community? Gangsters were still there but without himself and Birdman, and the core members of the gang around, outsiders would not think twice about coming in to take over. He needed to go back. He would go there tonight. He would spend most of the day with Christine and then round up two or three soldiers and go back. It had been foolish of him to think that he could stay away for so long. That was not the way to go.

He finished smoking and took a last look at the beautiful view. His stomach growled. He was hungry. He got on to the bike and gunned the engine. He would get some breakfast and then head home where Christine was waiting in his bed.

Corporal Crooks parked across from the apartment where Bambino was allegedly staying. The motorcycle wasn't there. He would wait there all day if he had to but something told him that it wouldn't come to that. Bambino was the party type, maybe he had gone to a strip club or a party and hadn't reached back home as yet. Then he would come home and sleep all day.

Not today.

Today he was in for a rude awakening. He looked over at his two friends. They had been rolling with him all night. He would have to share the money with them but it was all good. There would be many jobs after this. Detective Patterson, God bless his soul, always used to talk about how generous Marcel Chang was. There would be many more well-paying jobs from the wealthy business-man. He yawned and turned on the radio. He hoped Bambino had food in the house. He was hungry as hell.

Christine hummed as she got out of the shower and dried herself. Her stomach was rumbling. All that passionate sex with Bambino had thoroughly drained her body of its nutrients. She hoped Bambino returned soon. Incredibly, he had only been gone for forty-five minutes and she missed him like crazy. She padded to the bedroom and applied some lotion to her body. She then opened one of the dresser drawers to look for a T-shirt to put on. The drawer she opened didn't contain any clothes. There was a gun and some ammunition, a thick wad of cash held by an elastic band and a ring. Time stood still for Christine as she picked the ring up with a trembling hand.

No! No! God no! It can't be! It just cannot be!

It was.

Christine sat on the edge of the bed as her legs threatened to give way.

She would know this ring anywhere.

She had purchased it for her sister's last birthday. Almost maxed out her credit card to get it.

What was it doing in Bambino's drawer?

The answer, as painful and mind-boggling as it was, was crystal clear.

Her brain refused to accept it.

No there must be some explanation! Someone sold it to him! He found it somewhere!

But deep down she knew the dreadful truth.

She had met, fucked and fallen in love with her sister's murderer.

God must be playing a cruel joke on her.

Surely, he must know that this would be too much for her to bear.

Hot, salty tears rolled down her high cheekbones as her body shook mightily.

She opened her mouth to scream but only managed a croak.

She could hear the roar of a motorcycle engine.

Bambino had returned.

Chapter 28

"**H**e's here!" Corporal Crooks whispered urgently, as though afraid that Bambino would hear him and become aware of their presence. The men became alert and gripped their guns tightly as they watched Bambino ride into the complex. "Remember...we want him alive but if he won't surrender cut him down."

Bambino parked in front of the apartment and removed his helmet. The *feeling* was so intense that he felt light-headed. It had gotten progressively stronger as he made his way home and now it was at its apex. It had never failed him before. He was in grave danger. He should have heeded his intuition and not return. But he had so much money in the house and he needed it to get the ball rolling when he went back to Rosewater Meadows.

He glanced in his right rear view mirror.

He saw the tinted navy blue Toyota Corolla.

An unmarked police car he was sure.

They were here for him.

So that was it. The source of the *feeling.*

He could only assume it was the same set of cops that Deidre had told him had come into the community looking for him. He doubted it was an official visit. If it was, he would have been marked as a wanted man and he would have heard about it.

No. This was a personal visit. They had been looking for him on someone's behalf. Stinking, dirty corrupt cops. He despised them. At least he and other men like him had the decency not to pretend that they were something other than what they were: criminals. The cops hid behind their badges and committed as much crimes as the so-called criminals themselves.

His front door opened and he took his eyes off the mirror and looked up at Christine.

She was clad in a towel.

Her face bore an expression of horror and disbelief.

Something she was holding between her fingers glistened in the brilliant morning sunshine.

Bambino's heart sank.

It was a ring.

Her dead sister's ring.

She had found it.

She knew.

"Police! Don't bloodclaat move! Police!" Corporal Crooks shouted as he and the other two cops made their move. "Put up yuh hands high inna de air!"

They were still by the car, crouched with the doors open and their guns trained on Bambino. They were taking no chances. They knew that Bambino was a very dangerous man. The only reason why they hadn't killed him immediately was because of the money. Marcel Chang wanted him alive. Corporal Crooks' palms were sweating. Bambino had not even turned around his head to acknowledge them. He was still sitting there looking at the distraught young lady in the doorway.

Crazy motherfucker.

Christine's eyes were wide. She felt like she was filming an emotional action scene in a movie. She had almost peed herself when the men across the street pulled their weapons and started shouting at Bambino.

He didn't even flinch.

He was still looking at her.

He had seen the ring in her hand.

He knew that she knew.

His face was an emotional montage.

Sorrow. Regret. Anguish. Acceptance.

He was saying something to her.

"Run!" she heard Bambino shout as he pulled his gun and dove off the motorcycle in one smooth motion.

Christine screamed and ran back into the house as the guns started barking.

Bambino hit the ground hard. But he managed to keep a firm grip on his gun. He rolled over three times and got up in a shooting stance and squeezed off at the police officers. Two of his bullets shattered the windscreen and another buried itself in the shoulder of one of the cops. He kept moving sideways as he emptied his clip at the lawmen.

But he was no match for the three of them.

He was outgunned and outmanned.

The slugs from the law officers' weapons penetrated his skinny frame like eager little virgin dicks. They ripped large orifices in his body, severely damaging vital organs as they claimed his life; the same way he had claimed the lives of many others. He fell to the ground with a thud. The pain was excruciating. Death was upon him. His final thought was a very startling and painful realization. He had spent all of his eighteen years not caring whether he lived or died. Now, with death mere seconds away, he realized that he didn't want to die.

But it was too late.

The cops moved in on his body cautiously.

Corporal Crooks kicked Bambino's body.

Nothing.

He had kicked a corpse.

Bambino was dead.

Epilogue

Corporal Crooks and his team got in big trouble over the shooting. Miranda, Christine's best friend, had gotten caught in the crossfire. Her body had been found by Christine's car. She had exited the house to meet the cab she called to take her to work when the shooting had started. She had received a clean shot to the head, killing her instantly. Corporal Crooks and the other two policemen were suspended without pay pending an investigation. Miranda's aunt was married to a senior cop in the Jamaica Police Force so the heat was on. They would not receive the usual protection from the top brass this time. A vigorous probe into the circumstances surrounding the young woman's death was underway. Marcel Chang, as they had agreed, only paid him fifty thousand dollars for killing Bambino. The Rolex watch of sentimental value that Bambino had stolen from him had been badly damaged during the shootout. Crooks regretted taking the assignment. It had not been worth it. By the time he had given his two men their share of the money he had only been left with a paltry sum.

And now this. Who knows how long he would be suspended without pay and more importantly, depending on how the investigation into the shooting went, he could possibly face criminal charges. The thought of going to jail made him feel ill. He had put too many innocent people in jail. He wouldn't last a day before they killed him. He could not sit around and take that chance. He decided to flee the country.

Reaction on the street to Bambino's death was a mixed one. Peanuts, the don from Spanish Town, was upset about it. There was no way for him to recover the stolen cocaine now.

The people of Rosewater Meadows mourned him. He had defended the community well. A real soldier. The end of an era. Now thugs from Kirk Lane had taken over. They would be forced to change their political persuasion. Life in Rosewater Meadows would never be the same.

Deidre was in the country when her sister called her to tell her the news. She was crushed. She had really liked Bambino.

Nisha, after trying unsuccessfully to call Bambino for three days, learnt about his death from a guy who had just recently come to England from Jamaica. She overheard him talking about it to another guy while she was at the pub with a few friends. She had been stunned. It was devastating news. It was difficult to come to terms with the fact that she would never see Bambino again. Would never get the chance to have something real with him. She would mourn his death for a very long time.

Randy, the guy who had rented out the apartment to Bambino, was pleased that he had collected his rent upfront. He was also immensely pleased to find a bag filled with Jamaican and US currency in the bedroom closet. Bambino was cool but that was the kind of life he led. Live by the gun, die by the gun.

Christine was a wreck. The sequence of events leading from her sister's murder up to this point was just too much to handle. Nadine's murder; seeing Clive in action with another woman and his subsequent violent behaviour; meeting and falling in love with Bambino in very short order; learning that he was Nadine's murderer and practically seeing him get killed all in the same breath; and losing Miranda, her best friend, to an inadvertent bullet from the same cops who had killed Bambino, she was convinced that God had given her too much to deal with.

She suffered a nervous breakdown. Her mom, though they were not on good terms, came to Jamaica and took her back to England with her. After a brief stay in the hospital, therapy and a prescription of strong anti-depressants, Christine slowly became able to at least think about everything without feeling suicidal. She decided she would not go back to Jamaica. Not ever. There was nothing there for her except memories that if allowed, would drive her stark, raving mad. Her mom had told her that she could stay there as long as she needed to. She would do that until she got a job and her own place.

But she needed time.

Time to heal.

She knew deep down that she would never fully come to grips with the guilt she felt over falling in love with her sister's killer. Guilt that made her weep for hours on end. And the most inexplicable and hurtful part of it was that even now, with the knowledge that he had callously taken the life of the person that she had loved the most in the entire world, she still loved him.

All she could do was pray about it.

And hoped God listened and showed her a way to deal with it.

So she could be whole again.

Other K. SEAN HARRIS Titles:

NOVELS

- The Kingdom of Death
- Kiss of Death
- The Heart Collector
- Death Incarnate
- The Stud
- Merchants of Death: A Jamaican Saga of Drugs, Sex, Violence and Corruption

ANTHOLOGIES

- The Sex Files
- The Sex Files Volume 2
- Erotic Jamaican Tales
- More Erotic Jamaican Tales

LaVergne, TN USA
05 November 2010
203736LV00001B/11/P